Twisted Tales from the Desert

Twisted Tales from the Desert

Star Lady Tales Book 3

Mari Collier

Copyright (C) 2013 Mari Collier
Layout Copyright (C) 2016 Creativia

Published 2016 by Creativia
Book design by Creativia (www.creativia.org)
Cover art by http://www.thecovercollection.com/
This book is a work of fiction. Names, characters, places, and incidents are the product of the author's imagination or are used fictitiously. Any resemblance to actual events, locales, or persons, living or dead, is purely coincidental.
All rights reserved. No part of this book may be reproduced or transmitted in any form or by any means, electronic or mechanical, including photocopying, recording, or by any information storage and retrieval system, without the author's permission.
http://www.maricollier.com/

Contents

A Fairy Godmother Tale	1
Cruise Control	5
Rest in Peace	7
Forgotten Gods	14
Conversations With The Unknown	24
The Kiss	36
Bath Time	41
A Victim of Murder	43
Ghost Town Remodel	61
Between	72

A Fairy Godmother Tale

Ashley giggled as she emptied the fourth wine bottle into Heather's glass. "Maybe I should have bought more." She eased her slender body onto the ottoman and raised her glass.

"To us!" The five friends toasted each other.

Heather, Susan, and Meagan, were seated on the sofa. All three were carefully clad in California casual as befitted their rank. Linda was in the overstuffed chair nearest the sofa, her golden hair beauty-parlor perfect, but her outfit was a mishmash of definitely not designer abused $269.99 jeans, but authentic faded, frayed jeans that clung to every bump and curve, a designer blouse, and flip flops completed her outfit.

This was their semi-annual gathering to discuss their lives, joys, aspirations, politics, family, irks and irritations, employment, and significant others. They had thoroughly debated those subjects and were cautiously dancing around spirituality.

"What precisely does that mean?" asked Meagan, the confirmed atheist. "It sounds like a new word for religion, except you don't offend anyone by mentioning a specific religion or belief." Like the rest, her nails gleamed, carefully applied makeup enhanced her features.

"Oh, no," the rest were quick to chorus.

"It means that you are on a search for your inner self to connect with the life force of the universe."

"And what, Susan, is 'life force' if not a euphemism for God?"

"Really, Meagan, you can't deny the benefits of meditation for health and inner growth." Ashley was horrified. "Why even doctors acknowledge the power of prayer for the very ill."

The others rushed in with their own explanations.

"What utter rot!" Meagan exploded.

The four stared at her in disbelief.

Heather stood. "Meagan, I have $25,000.00 dollars that says you will notice a difference if you practice it." Heather had succeeded in the market place and had married an older, extremely wealthy ex-stockbroker who promptly had the good sense to drop dead when the SEC wanted to investigate his personal dealings with a well-known oilman.

"Do you mean I'm supposed to sit around for ten or twenty minutes a day thinking about some deity to achieve self-awareness and a feeling of peace?" Inwardly she gritted her teeth. She hadn't mentioned her company would be downsizing in six months. If she didn't find employment right away, she'd lose her house and car.

"If I did try it," and she stressed did, "and reported that nothing happened, would you renege?"

"No, I wouldn't. You must meditate at least fifteen minutes a day upon a spiritual entity for six months. You can report the results when we're together again. I'll be prepared to write you a check."

"Are you dictating the entity?"

"No, you pick the spiritual guide or entity, but you do have to name the entity of mediation."

Meagan considered. $25,000.00 would cover three months worth of living expenses with money left over. By that time she would have another place of employment. She racked her brains trying to think of something less offensive to her sensibilities.

"Well," Heather challenged, "do you accept or do you concede that we are correct?"

"You're wrong." Meagan snapped.

"So prove it." The rest applauded Heather's response. "You may even choose yoga, Meagan, as long as it isn't an inanimate object."

The last glass of wine interfered with Meagan's brain cells and nothing suitable seemed to surface. She needed a fairy godmother at a time like this. On the theory that more wine would be beneficial, she emptied the glass in one swallow. She needed someone equipped with a wand that could make things right. Meagan straightened, and sat primly like a little girl in a pew.

"Very well, I choose the Fairy Godmother, an appropriate mythical figure devised by a man."

They looked at her stunned.

"But what spiritual values are embedded in a Fairy Godmother?" Ashley was horrified.

"The conditions are that I meditate on anything I wished except an inanimate object." She controlled an effort to laugh. What an easy $25,000.00 this would be. If she found employment immediately, she could afford a new luxury car and pay off some of those credit cards.

"Oh, I nearly forgot. How does one meditate? I know how to set the timer, but what do I do; sit with my hands folded, look upward, or what?"

"Meagan, you can sit, stand, jog, assume the lotus position, or recline. You should be wary about the latter as falling asleep doesn't count." Heather was becoming shrewish. "We're taking your word on this as it is."

"I can always sit up a video." Meagan smiled at them. "Do I need incense or bells?"

"Yes, if that sets the mood; otherwise, no. Sometimes complete quiet is more beneficial. Crystals and scented oils are used to set the mood." Ashley tried to interject a calm response.

Heather would have none of it. "You're afraid we're right. Either take the bet now or forget it."

"I'll take it. I'll even set up the video and you can watch every minute of it. When I win, I'll cater our next meeting."

Everything that could possibly go wrong did. Meagan lost her job, but catered the next meeting as a way to celebrate and collect her $25,000.00. She did not find another position. Her ARM mortgage reset and the payments were impossible to meet. The stock market tanked along with the housing market. She shunned her friends and tried selling her house, but no takers. Her 401K and stock purchases were worthless.

Within one year, she was reduced to a sleeping bag under a cement overpass and a cart filled with her possessions. Today, she'd eaten at a mission and pocketed a protein bar at a drugstore while paying for another one. The two bars were her dinner tonight and breakfast in the morning.

"It's too damn bad there really isn't a fairy godmother," she muttered as she returned from the bushes after relieving herself.

"Here I am, dearie."

Meagan looked at the woman who had materialized in front of her. Her graying blonde hair was long and flowing, the tiara on her head wobbled to one side, the satin, white gown clung to her figure and flowed to the ground to cover any footwear. The golden wand and huge jewels on her fingers did not look like fakes; neither did the large, clear stone in her pendant. Her brown eyes were beginning to dim with age and there were wrinkles around her mouth and eyes. The neck was crisscrossed with diamond puckers of skin.

"Where were you when I needed you?"

"Tut, tut, my dear, tonight your prayers are answered. Tomorrow all will be as it is now, but tonight you'll attend the academy awards and the dinner and dance afterward. Of course, you will have to leave at midnight."

"In these clothes? They wouldn't let me in the door."

"Very easily taken care of, my dear, plus I supply the transportation, a nice Bentley or Mercedes. I won't even make you catch the mice like dear Cinderella had to do."

"One night? I need a house, a job, my clothes."

"Don't be silly. I am the Fairy Godmother. I do balls, not jobs."

Cruise Control

Cruise control is one of the marvels of modern automotive engineering. Once you are at the speed limit, you simply set the control and it takes over. A blind man could drive the car for all the effort it takes to hold the speed constant. Maybe that is the reason a blind man by the name of Ralph Teetor invented it.

It was for me (a frugal person at heart) a rather expensive option. Not as bad as when it first came out and was limited to your top-of-the line automobiles like Chrysler Imperial. Cruise control remains an option for fewer and fewer vehicles. All I wanted was an automobile to take me from point A to point B at a reasonable cost. Said cost, of course, required a decent mileage. As you can see, my life style became as dull as my accounting profession.

Today many of your newer cars come equipped with all the bells and whistles including cruise control and excellent mileage. That description applies to my shiny, smells-like-a-new-car-interior vehicle. Your self-righteous environmentalist will expound, "I never exceed fifty-five miles per hour to save gasoline and leave less of a carbon imprint." Well, fine and dandy, but the speed limit on my regularly traveled highway is seventy to eighty miles per hour. Twiddling along at fifty-five could induce road rage in the person behind a slow moving vehicle. Not something one needs with trucks and autos whizzing by. The most compelling argument for possessing cruise control is that setting the speed control saves gasoline money.

How you may ask? It's simple. The cruise control creates an even flow to keep the speed at where you have set it. If you are driving at seventy miles per hour and try to keep it at seventy miles per hour, you need to keep checking your speed along with the traffic on either side, in front, and behind you. If you check your mileage at the end of a trip or a stretch of road and you've maintained a seventy mile per hour average, it means you've driven under and over, adjusting your gas pedal accordingly. Sorry, you can't do it as efficiently as a machine.

With the cruise control on, I found I could sit back and enjoy watching the scenery instead of the speedometer. That chore of driving became relaxing. I set the cruise control and went sailing down Highway 10. There were buildings, rocks and greenery off in the distance that I had never seen before. I heaved a sigh at the ease with which I clipped off the miles. It became a soothing drive, a soothing, relaxing morning; so relaxing I fell asleep.

Now I'm on a journey that never ends, cruising at seventy miles an hour on a road filled with madmen and madwomen as punishment for my stupidity. It's a never ending replay of what we did wrong. At least I went out with a bang.

Rest in Peace

Dad didn't really grasp the concept of Rest In Peace when he passed on. True, life around him was always disruptive, but since his demise, things became worse. Things like banging doors in the middle of the night are a real bummer when you're trying to sleep away the wine buzz in your head. Those late night trips to the bathroom take on a whole new aspect when ramming your big toe into a piece of furniture that is supposed to be against the far wall—not in the middle of your direct path. In real life Dad would throw things whenever he was upset and yell; especially yell at the offender whether present or not.

At least he can't yell anymore or if he is yelling, no one hears him. But throwing things? He didn't stop. A physical manifestation that is totally impossible according to the scientific world. Science needs to revisit that issue. You try sitting peacefully at the table enjoying your dinner and then glasses and plates start crashing in the kitchen. Consequently, I've switched to all plastic, but even those will shatter when thrown hard enough.

I really hadn't wanted to return to the little desert town that I ran from as a young adult, but I needed time to lick my wounds. Brian, my ex, had decided that he needed his space and that we were through. Considering the arguing we had done every night for years, I didn't even bother to bat my big blues at him. Not only did he divorce me, but my company downsized. During the divorce, Brian managed to be awarded part of my "golden" parachute on the basis that his bad back made him partially disabled. Our house was sold as part of the divorce settlement. Of course, with home prices sinking all over the nation, the price was far less than he anticipated. It also meant I needed to conserve my money. I did splurge on new clothes and a blond hairdo before returning home.

At least it was a refuge while I redefined my life. Unfortunately, Dad was the only living parent and we differed on politics.

To escape his constant bickering, I took a course in creative writing at the local community college. That's where I was when the police paged me out of class. It seems Dad suffered a stroke while driving and had been involved in a one vehicle crash. At first they thought he was drunk, then realized it was a medical problem caused by a massive stroke. His abilities to move, talk clearly, or swallow were destroyed.

The hospital in Joshua Tree, California wanted to send him down below to Palm Springs for intensive treatment, but I already had his living will and he had forbidden any heroic measures or feeding tubes. His orders were clear.

"Let me die in peace and at home if possible."

The medical professionals patiently explained that without a tube in his stomach for feeding he would die. I agreed with them, but I honored my father's wishes. Hospice transported him home.

The Hospice people came every day to move him, bathe him. A visiting nurse made sure the liquid IV was correct. I spent my days checking on him and the nights in a chair beside him. Most of the time his breathing was slow and labored and his eyes closed. Whenever he noticed me, Dad would rouse briefly and whisper, "id." His face would turn red and his eyes closed again as he resumed his labored breathing.

Now Dad was never one for philosophical musings about the Id. He was more of a beer, football, and motorcycle kind of guy. His choice of words, or rather a word, baffled me. To wile away the time, I worked crossword puzzles. When one definition asked for a cockney's home, the explanation hit me. Dad wasn't referring to the Id. He meant hid.

The next time he roused to say id, I clasped his hand and asked, "Do you mean you hid something, Dad?"

For one moment his face cleared and he blinked his eyes.

"Eg," was his next utterance and his eyes closed.

This was just as puzzling as the first word, but obviously the added h would mean heg or maybe hag. One certainly can't hide a nonexistent heg, but if he had hidden a hag, you'd think she'd object or start to smell. I gave up trying to figure it out.

By nightfall his breathing slowed. Suddenly his eyes blinked open, then his mouth widened, and he hoarsely whispered, "Eg, no, eg, id eg…" Before he could say more, his head fell back. Whatever he was trying to say died with him. I called the Hospice number I'd been given and sat down to wait for the professionals. Dad was buried within the week.

The first two weeks after the funeral was filled with paperwork, cleaning, and clearing the main closet. In the garage were his vehicles that needed the title changed prior to selling and his tools. The Hospice people suggested grief group therapy or a therapist. I'm a great one to direct others into counseling when needed, but the word therapist has always put me off. Remove the first three letters and you are left with rapist. Trust me; some of my friends that took advantage of the therapist solution realized the truth of the spelling.

All the closet clearing, dusting, and mopping turned up nothing of particular value that was hidden away. Dad's methods were as straightforward as his life; other than the beer drinking at times.

As I accumulated articles for the yard sale the doors began banging and things moving. One day this went on from morning to midnight. Lights would snap on for no reason. To fight back, I bought earplugs and a sleeping mask. Then I called a realty agent.

The realty agent had hair a little too black, but in the desert heat he wore a white shirt with a tie. I suspected he loosened it or removed it the minute he was not with a client, but, hey, he was here with said tie. Not that the housing market was moving. Actually, houses had now been sitting for seven months rather than six, but banging doors, flying objects, and lights going on and off were enough to make me a motivated seller.

They also proved too much for the agent. On the first banging door, I tried to laugh it off as the desert wind banging something against the house. The second time, I exclaimed, "Oh my, that poor bird almost knocked itself out on the window." The agent's face was turning red when a salt shaker went flying by and the kitchen light blinked off an on.

"What is going on here?" It was a rhetorical question addressed to the wall.

Then a potted plant hit him in the back of the head. He turned on me.

"Miss Danbury, I don't know what you are trying to pull, but you need another agent, one who appreciates practical jokes." His face was a mottled tan and white as he stormed out of the house, loosening his tie as he ran.

My neighbor, Jeri Taylor, was heading her rose bushes. When she heard the door slam, she turned and watched him sprint to his car, fumble at the door, and roar away. She swiped a gray lock of hair back on her forehead and turned towards me with a puzzled look on her face.

"Linda, wasn't that your realty person? What ailed him?"

From inside the house came the sound of the contents of the silverware drawer hitting the floor and cabinet doors slamming. I knew it wasn't polite, but there was no way I could answer her. I simply rushed back inside to deal with the mess.

"All right, Dad, settle down. I won't move until I find what you hid." I didn't know if he could hear me or would listen to me, but at least the doors quit banging while I picked up the silverware.

Jeri's voice startled me. "Well, it looks like Walt is still capable of throwing a fit, and you, my dear, look like you could use a nice glass of ice tea. Shall we go over to my place?"

"Yes, your place," was all I could think of to say.

She didn't exactly lead me by the hand, but I don't remember walking there. I came back to reality when I slid into her kitchen chair.

"I really must apologize for following you into your house like that, but I was afraid you were in danger. I had no idea Walt had become a poltergeist. It's better to discuss things here." She held two glasses to the ice maker, pulled the pitcher from her fridge, and filled the glasses.

She handed one to me and then sat in the chair on the opposite side of the table. "How long has this been going on, and what is it that Walt hid?" Jeri swiped the offending lock of hair back from her forehead.

I almost cried. Until now I hadn't realized how stressful the last few weeks had been. Here was our retired, comfortably padded, neighbor talking like an angry spirit roaming the house was normal.

"I don't know. I didn't even know he hid anything until I figured out he meant hid instead of 'Id' like he kept saying. When I asked him what he hid, he said 'eg or egg', maybe he meant 'ag.' Eg with an h in front of it didn't make any sense and neither does hag. Just to make sure, I checked in the fridge, but the one carton of eggs contained eggs, nothing else."

"Have you gone through everything?"

"No, just the surface things like his clothes, the tools he left strewed about, his truck, and motorcycle. Now I have to start digging in all the things he had stored from the time Mom was alive."

"Well, if you need any help, you let me know."

"I will."

My promise was half-hearted at best. I simply didn't want anyone going through Mom's private papers and photos. I hated to admit how much I had missed my mother these last five years: She of the blithe spirit and gentle laugh. She was able to laugh at all my dad's foibles. I knew I'd be sitting there weeping as I went through her things.

And weep I did as Dad hadn't thrown out anything. He'd packed everything of hers away and stored it in the shed out back. There was nothing, absolutely nothing resembling an egg worth anything. Whatever he hid, however, must be in the house as nothing in the shed or garage fit what he tried to tell me. It was only when I returned to the house that doors would open and things would fly.

The work and the summer heat began preying on me and I knew I needed a break. I called Vern. I know, I hadn't mentioned him, but he was in the creative fiction class with me. He's my age, his brown hair is thinning a bit, he wears glasses, and weighs a bit more than he did in high school, but don't we all?

We had a great time with dinner at the Inn, a play at the Twentynine Palms Theatre, and then a drink afterward. We decided it was best to go to one of our homes if we were going to have another drink. Since my home was closest, mine was chosen. We'd have a drink and chat. Big mistake! Dear old Dad went into one of his rages that night.

Vern became thirsty during the middle-of-the-night and traipsed out to the kitchen for a drink of water. After all, we both downed several glasses of wine and dehydration can occur. He was unsure of which cabinet held the glasses and started opening doors.

Dad let fly with the silverware drawer and then started heaving the kitchen chairs. All of which scored a direct hit on Vern. Unlike the salesman, Vern didn't bother to ask what was going on. The last I heard of him, he was picked up by the police for running down the middle of Amboy Road in just his t-shirt. Needless to say, our romance was over.

My head was a bit large the next day, but I finally began cleaning the kitchen. Maybe that would settle dear old Dad down. Hah! He added flying pots and pans to his repertoire. While balancing on a stool to reach the highest shelf, a pot hit my knee.

"That's it." I yelled at him. "Either you settle down and let me look for whatever you hid in my own way or I move out and sell this place as is at a loss!"

I grabbed my purse and stormed out of the house to give him an opportunity to calm down. Three blocks down the road and I realized I was driving fast enough to compete in the Indy 500. I slowed to a crawl and drove to the largest grocery store in town for a six pack of iced coffee and a new crossword puzzle book.

The checkout person smiled at me and said, "Hi, you're Walt's daughter, right? I was at the funeral with my mom."

She must have seen my puzzled look and explained. "Mom was Brenda Crandall when she went to high school with you. I went because Walt was always so nice when he came in here."

I looked at the pretty, blond Southern California girl and figured Dad would have been really nice.

"That's $9.68. Would you like a Mega Lottery ticket? Your dad used to come in once a week to buy five tickets."

That was a surprise. Dad never really gambled, but he would buy scratch tickets and lottery tickets occasionally.

"Uh, I don't think so. The odds are too great."

The cashier smiled at me. "That's true, but somebody bought a winning ticket here the week before Walt died. So far he or she hasn't turned up and everybody is wondering who it is."

By this time my mouth was hanging open and my mind a jumble of thoughts. If he had left off the first letter of hid, maybe he left off the first and last letter of Mega. Awkwardly, I pulled out my billfold and then a ten dollar bill.

"Did my dad ever say anything else?" Like maybe he won ran through my mind.

She laughed. "Yes, he used to say that he had to win big to make you change your political affiliation so he could quit yelling at you."

I ran for my car with the girl shouting after me, "Ma'am, your change, your groceries."

My feet were still running when I hit the kitchen door.

"Dad, calm down. I know what I'm looking for now. You've hid a Mega Lottery ticket."

The kitchen cabinets and the china cabinet were easy to eliminate as there was only one place in each that he would hide anything; like the highest shelf to keep out the children. Next I went through the drawers in the end tables, coffee table, and entertainment unit. At first Dad quit throwing things, but as

I went through each unit and found nothing resembling a lottery ticket, he began turning over lamps, chairs and pulling out the drawers again. I finally went back to his ledger in the coffee table drawer. After all, it was it the same drawer where he had stored "his" remote.

I lifted the ledger out and held it over the coffee table, shaking it as I opened it. A lottery ticket with five rows of numbers floated out and down to the table.

"I found it, Dad. Rest In Peace."

The huge recliner quit moving across the floor.

Of course, I still haven't changed my political affiliation, but I'm weighing my options.

Forgotten Gods

"Look at it. It's a desert iguana!" Stacie pointed at the huge, beige rock boulder with a wind and sand carved sculpture of a lizard perched on top.

The brilliant desert heat, sweat running from every pore, sore feet, sore muscles, everything was forgotten as she pointed to their find. "The tail is straight. It's tremendous. How did it come into existence? Darn these straps." She tore at the camera straps hanging at her side.

"I thought we were taking photos of flora and fauna. That means vegetable matter or living creatures, not wind-sculpted ones." Bill was used to her flights of fancy, but why become excited about something that gave the impression of a lizard?

Stacie aimed her camera at the stone lizard. "It looks like a desert iguana. See even the side is pinkish like it is in the breeding season. Let's look and see if the other side is the same." She was taking more shots as she moved to go around the boulder.

Bill stared at her back. Had she really found something that would sell to a national magazine?

"It is! It is!" She shouted and came back around the boulder, a huge smile on her wind burnt face. Bill could imagine those big brown eyes sparkling behind the dark glasses.

"Plus, on the other side, the ledge juts out farther and makes it look like he's resting on a platform. I can't wait to see him in the moonlight."

"And how do you know it is a 'he'?"

Stacie's smile disappeared and her face became serious. "I just do. I want to spend the night here and take pictures in the different lighting. It's almost time to make camp anyway. We can count the living plants and creatures that are here. We've completed the assigned days and distance."

Mark caught up with them, his skinny frame belying his strength and stamina. Like the others, a bandana and a field cap covered his hair. "I told you that taking the other way over that small mountain rather than going the designated way was going to throw us off. The good news is that according to the GPS and headquarters this is an area that hasn't been tabulated in years. If our supplies warrant, we are to spend another day cataloging the plants and creatures."

"That avalanche stopped us from going the normal route out, but the way down saved us a day, so, yes, we have enough supplies if the truck is headed here."

"Zoe back tracked and came this way. She will be here within the hour."

"Good, you two can circle the perimeter and do the counting. I'm staying right here." Stacie took a swig out of her water bottle.

"Careful, you can see the vegetation is mostly creosote which means there are lots of ground bees." Bill was still baffled by her fascination.

"Which are harmless desert creatures," she added. "You're just upset because I found something more interesting. If some natural history or hiking journal takes one of the pictures of the stone iguana, we haven't broken any contract, and may earn enough to celebrate."

"We are out here to see if the range of plants and mammals are migrating north due to climate change and if they are adapting."

"Don't use that lecturing tone on me, William Mason. I am not in your classroom. Anyone can see those creosote bushes are old."

Stacie turned her back and began the slow process of taking shots of the lizard from different angles. "I think I'll climb up there on the other side." She walked off, her hiking boots making her swaying hips look ridiculous.

Mark grinned at Bill. "You two don't mix too well. Why do you keep going into far-a-way places together and dating like you are serious?"

They deposited their backpacks by hanging them on two of the sturdier creosote limbs.

"Because she keeps getting the damn pictures that people want and I keep finding the plant life the biologists drool over. We're both much more civilized in an urban setting and seem to agree on everything. Let's see what we can find out in the area to South."

"Might as well. Zoe said it would take her an hour to hook up with us."

They all met beside the truck as Zoe pulled in. She stepped out with a big smile on her round face. "It's a good thing you sent me those coordinates. This is several miles from our intended rendezvous, but it's impressive. How long do you think time took to carve that out?" She pointed at the lizard.

"What is it with you women?" Bill was muttering.

"Are you still mad about the handiwork of nature?" Stacie was perplexed. Bill usually agreed with her ideas of a good shoot.

"It's wrong." Mark was squinting as he looked at it. "It shouldn't be there. There aren't any other boulders around here with that beige and grey color. If it was carved by water, it was eons ago and the wind would have worn down the features more."

"Maybe the Native Americans had a hand in sculpting it."

"I doubt it. This is a nasty part of the Colorado Desert. That's why the creosote bushes are so thick. There may be water down below, but nothing else is really here. In fact this whole area is wrong."

Zoe laughed. It looks like a normal slice of the desert to me. If you added a little rain there are probably desert blooms. Did you find any belly buttons?"

"No, there are no flowers. It's nothing but creosote. No cheese bushes, no signs of any spent flowering plants, nor any other scrub brush that usually appears. There's a wash on the other side of the East line of creosote bushes, but no sign of a smoke tree or anything else."

"That proves nothing. Let's get our gear out and see if this truck doesn't offer some sort of shade until the evening starts to cool things down."

Mark shrugged. "Okay, Bill, but it still isn't natural. I can't wait to see what kind of wild life appears tonight and in the morning."

Zoe had boosted herself up in the camper and was handing out chairs. "What's not natural other than it being abnormally warm for the middle of May?"

"That the creosote bushes have been here a long time may not be surprising, but look at them. They circle this boulder. There was that trail coming in here and there is one going out the other side in perfect alignment. Plants don't grow that way and I've never heard of anyone domesticating creosote bushes other than those that are volunteers on someone's property and the owners clipped and shaped it."

"Well, maybe the early hunter gatherers used it as a place of meditation or star gazing."

They were taking the camp equipment that Zoe handed down and setting it up.

"You know that's not likely. Did you see any artifacts on the surface?" Bill was skeptical, but he had seen the bushes. They did form an amphitheater.

"Why isn't it possible?" Stacie asked and continued. "Native Americans in Mexico and farther south had temple centers."

"Right, but they built temples with lots of sculpture and had the area around it paved with blocks of stone. There weren't isolated sculptures." Bill felt obligated to refute her.

"So these people hadn't learned the technique of temple building."

"That's it, folks." Zoe jumped down from the tailgate and put it up. "Let's fix something to eat before it gets any later. There's going to be a full moon tonight so you should have a good view of any nocturnal creatures." She pointed at the white circle visible on the grey horizon.

It was one of those clear, cloudless desert evening when the full moon spreads a white light over the earth. Anything blocking the light becomes a dark, mirror image on the sand resembling the silhouette art of long ago. By midnight they called a halt. Wildlife had been scarce except for a few jack rabbits, one lonely owl and a cricket croaking somewhere. Coyotes could be heard in the distance, but none came close.

"I hope the hunting is better in the morning." Bill grinned at them as he rose and stretched. "I haven't seen any insects either. Just those burrow holes under the creosote and that's probably desert iguanas."

"I hope they don't mean snakes."

"Aw, come on, Zoe. You are in the wrong business if you are going to freak out over snakes, but if it bothers you, I can pull my gear closer."

"You're such a comfort, Mark, but thank you, no. I'm sleeping in the camper. There's just enough room for one to be comfortable." She let down the back and hoisted herself up.

"Goodnight all."

The rest shook out their bedrolls and spread them out in an area that was flat. Most people scrape out the ground for a sleeping bag, but they did not wish to disturb the desert floor. If there were seeds just below the surface waiting for rain, scraping the earth would obliterate them.

"It's so damn bright you almost need something over your eyes for it to be dark enough to sleep." Bill was still grumbling. He found this place disturbing, but hadn't been able to put it into words. There was nothing concrete, nothing out of the extraordinary for a desert other than the stone lizard and the arrangement of the creosote bushes, neither was enough to make it dangerous.

Stacie awoke that night with the sound of humming in her ears. It was haunting, calling her, and she rolled over to shut her eyes against the bright moonlight and her ears against the sound that summoned her.

She found herself walking to the other side of the boulder, her hips and shoulders swaying with the sound. No one was on the other side. Where is that sound coming from? Could there be small holes in the boulder and the wind was whispering to her? But there was no wind. She looked up at the lizard that seemed to be looking down at her. She closed her eyes as she swayed with the humming and the soft, desert night air caressed her bare arms.

Was that the sound of rocks rolling? Stacie opened her eyes to look upward. She shook her head in two quick snaps and blinked her eyes. The lizard couldn't disappear. The moonlight was playing tricks on her. She looked again and arms were around her. She was thrown to the ground.

Before she could get her breath, the heavy weight was on her, pinning her, almost suffocating her. She tried to fight, but all she could do was attempt to roll back and forth. She felt her shorts and briefs being drug downward, cold stone separating her legs, and something hard plowed into her inner being.

"So many once visited me," hummed in her head. "It is the planting time. At harvest time you will return and bury your eggs here."

Stacie felt a claw take her hand and dig in the dirt. "The new ones will emerge in front of me."

The thing slammed into her again and seemed to twist as burning pain shot through her. And reality fled into darkness.

Stacie woke while the rising sun exploded rose and pink streamers across the desert sky. She was gasping and panting. She brought herself up into a sitting position. Then she looked upward.

The stone lizard was on the top of the flattened area. The ground around her was the same. She wet her lips and stood before pulling up her clothes. What did she tell the others? That she had been raped by a wind sculpted statue. They would think her insane or that she had dreamt an erotic fantasy. The soft light of early morning illuminated everything. There were no other footprints.

Wouldn't something that heavy leave a mark or the tail the signs of something drug in the sand? There was nothing except where a small, scratched out hole had been dug near the boulder. She realized there was sand on her left hand and under her fingernails. She covered her face with her hands. It was a dream. It had to have been a dream. She felt the grains of sand from her left hand scrape her face and she brushed them away before walking back around the bolder.

"Ah, there you are." It was Zoe. "The rest went off in the other direction. I'll take yours. Why don't you..." Her voice trailed off.

"Is there anything wrong, Stacie?"

"No, why would there be?" Her words came through gritted teeth and she turned away and then turned back.

"Is there enough fresh water for wash up?"

"Use the hand sanitizers. They're in the blue chest." Zoe walked around the boulder and towards the creosote bushes, her back stiff against what she considered a rebuff.

Screw you too, Stacie thought.

* * *

Once they were back at the university, they compiled their notes, wrote down their findings, filed them with the proper department, and went their separate ways for the summer. Stacie was thankful she no longer needed to interact with them. Bill called a couple times to ask about the photographs. She did not return his calls and no more came for a month. She deleted every photograph from the memory card as though expunging the image expunged the event, but she could not expunge the morning vomiting. She refused to make an appointment with a doctor. For what purpose? Stone could not beget flesh. Her afternoons were spent at the University writing class outlines and coordinating schedules with the necessary time for research. This time the Biology and Paleontology departments wanted a more northerly zone.

By August the vomiting had ceased and she regained her weight. Stacie assumed that now she was free of the incident and she eagerly prepared for the resumption of her classes and research projects. She called Bill to see what he was planning for a Labor Day weekend. It was time to resume her normal life rather than hide away from prying eyes. They set up a time to meet for dinner on Friday evening and would plan the rest of the weekend there.

That evening she dressed in her wicked red gown and black pumps, filled up her gas tank and headed for the desert. It was as though an innate force had taken over her mind. She stopped once for gas, water, and food. The water she stored in the back of her auto and the food she ate. She was exhausted by morning and unable to reach her destination. She drove into the first motel she saw before collapsing and wrecking her auto.

She woke later in the afternoon, the same urgency driving her on. Nothing mattered except that she return to the base of that obscenity.

Stacie grasped the steering wheel and inserted her key.

"This is insanity," she yelled at the driving force in her mind. "I cannot get there in these clothes or this vehicle. It will stall in the sand and everything in it dies or rusts away. You may kill me, but you've lost again." She began to sob as she drove out of the parking lot without returning the electronic key to the front desk.

She found herself driving into a small mall. When she left she was clothed in a long sleeved shirt, socks, boots, jeans, and a straw hat. Her next stop was an auto agency. She drove out in a large, four-wheel drive pickup loaded with her supplies and began barreling down Highway 10 towards the Joshua Tree National Park.

That night the stars were brilliant and she held her stomach against the hunger pangs. She had stopped for water and to eat the last power bar but it wasn't sufficient. This time when the cell phone rang she answered it.

"Stacie, where are you? I was mad as hell when you didn't show, but you haven't been home or at work. What's going on?"

"Bill, I'm out here. I can't fight it. I have to go back. I-I don't know how to stop it." Her words came out between sobs and she ended the connection. The cell rang again and she turned it off before falling asleep for a few hours.

She woke at half light and began driving again. How she would be able to find her way to the sculpture was unclear in her mind, but the truck continued forward. She tried to will herself to stop, to shut off the motor, but she found it was impossible. She closed her eyes and felt the truck swerve. Instinct made her open her eyes and keep the vehicle from crashing or turning over. *I can't stop this* ran through her mind.

Stacie knew the entire scenario was insane. She did not know the coordinates, but the vehicle continued upwards and toward a high mound of rocks. She did not know how far she was off the main road, but the scenery was beginning to look vaguely familiar as she went upward and the gas gauge went downward.

"I'll never get out of here!" She was screaming at the windshield as though that would transmit her thoughts, her words, her desperation.

Night was drawing closer as she rolled into the level space surrounded by creosote bushes on either side of the track that served as a road. The huge boulder set in the center pulled her onward. She knew what was there and she could not stop.

Stacie drove to the side of the boulder and stumbled out of the truck. Her legs were trembling as she walked to the side where the stone iguana looked outward with regal grace.

"I don't want to be here." And the words did no good. She felt her pelvis bones move and the pain drove her to her knees. To relieve the pressure she pulled down her jeans and then her briefs. With her hands, she began scooping away at the sand. The throbbing noise began in her head and grew louder and louder. The air around her vibrated and the pain nearly doubled her over. Somehow she went into a squatting position and made her muscles push downward as her pelvis bones seemed to widen and her abdomen muscles contracted. The pain drove her head into the sand and she felt something leave her body. She put her hands on the sand and pushed her shoulders up when something else seem to gush out with the last contraction.

Stacie was sobbing and she stood, pulling up the briefs and jeans, not caring if they were ruined. She couldn't bring herself to look at what was in the depression she had dug. She staggered toward the truck while a noise screeched in her head.

"No, no, come back! You must cover them. You are to be my consort and tend them. They will die without you. Die like the others and I'll be forgotten again."

Stacie yanked the door opened and boosted herself into the seat. The key was still in the ignition where she left it. She clapped her hands over her ears, screaming her protests.

"I don't care. I'll die if I stay here and that—that whatever it is will die too."

The motor turned over and she backed the truck out. Her teeth were clamped together. She had to do this slowly or she would be stuck in the sand and die here. She managed to get five miles back towards where she had left the main road when she realized her gas gauge was becoming dangerously low. Nausea overwhelmed her and she stopped before turning off the gas and leaving the cab. Once outside she vomited. This, she knew was dangerous. The desert was still hot and she would dehydrate. She grabbed the water bottle and drank. Don't take just sips she reminded herself. People died in the desert from dehydration and there would still be water in their canteens. She looked down at the tire tracks from the truck she had made coming in and swallowed. Night was covering the earth and she could not follow tracks in the dark. If she turned off the air conditioner tomorrow and left the windows open she would conserve what little gas she had left. She would be closer to well traveled trails, but no one knew she was here. If she ran out of gas, she'd have to wait until nightfall again before walking out. There was no GPS unit in the truck and her cell was useless here.

"I will not let that monstrosity kill me." She did not shout, but saying it aloud strengthened her resolve as she climbed back in the truck. I'll sleep tonight and tomorrow go as far as I can, she decided.

Stacie woke just as the sun spilled golden light over the world. She yawned, stretched, and rubbed at her neck. She looked up at the rearview mirror as she started to open the door to find a place more private than the side of the truck. She froze. The stone lizard was almost upon her. She began shaking as she turned the key. There wasn't enough gas to run very far. I won't submit to that again she thought and rolled forward, and then put the gear in reverse to turn around.

"If I die out here, so do you!" She was shouting, hoping that thing could hear her. While she turned, she considered her possibilities. Hitting it at a high speed wasn't possible in this sand, but low speed was and this was a huge truck with four-wheel drive for the desert. In the distance she saw sand billowing in the air as though another vehicle was on this trail.

"At least they'll see sand flying from an impact. My bones won't bleach out here," she muttered, and put the truck into low gear to move forward.

The stone lizard stood, opening its short arms to welcome her back. The truck rammed the stone middle and the lizard swayed back and forth. The truck seemed to squat to gather strength and continued to press against the stone mass. Stacie knew the bumper was ruined. It didn't matter. She pushed the gas pedal lower and the huge body crashed backward, trying to turn out of her way. The tail snapped off and the lizard toppled sideways into the boulders, smashing its upper left arm. The arm became small stones that rolled to the ground.

The humming was back in her head, pleading for help, for workers to return it to its former glory and majesty. "Yours are the new ones. Those crawling creatures are but their degenerate descendants."

"Fat chance!" Stacie was still yelling as she put the truck in reverse.

"Slow, slow," she repeated to herself. "You cannot go fast in this sand." She didn't know how far she would get, but that billowing sand seemed to be closer. If she died it would be nowhere near that—that thing.

She had the truck turned and ready to drive out when Zoe's familiar white and green truck appeared as it headed straight toward her. Bill stuck his head out of the passenger window and waved.

She was still shaking when Bill opened the door and pulled her into his arms.

"What the hell are you doing out here? And what is that thing?"

"It's that stone lizard. It was after me." She looked up at him.

"Bill, how did you know?"

"You've been acting weird all summer, and then when you didn't show for our date I figured something was wrong. I called to give you a chance to explain. You said you had to go back and there was only one place for you to return."

Stacie closed her eyes and tears spilled down. The humming was gone. The sounds from the desert and from the trucks' motors were all she heard. She was free.

Conversations With The Unknown

"What are they?" asked Darla as Kevin pulled the box of parts out from under the wooden shelf.

"I can't see. Shine that light down here."

He sorted through the dust covered box. The various tubes, Bakelite cover, boards, and faded gray rubber coated wires were dust-coated brown from their long sojourn in the shed.

"Hell, it looks like old radio parts. Like when instead of buying a radio in the store, you bought the parts and built your own. See, this box has a plug-in for an ear. Only one person at a time could listen to the radio."

"You are kidding me, aren't you?"

He grinned. "Nope. This could be fun. Let's keep it. I'm just wondering who it belonged to. Your grandmother wasn't very old when they moved here, was she?"

"No she wasn't but four or five. It must have been her father's." Darla pushed a lock of dark brown hair back behind her ear. "You can work on that nasty thing later; much later. We need to haul everything out and sort it for selling. Maybe we should just call in a dealer. This stuff is ancient."

Reluctantly, Kevin put the box back under the shelf. This would be a challenge like he hadn't had since putting together his first computer. The directions weren't in the box. It was obvious that someone had taken it apart when the improved models came out. He looked and saw Darla's trim figure struggling with an oversized box to position it near the door.

"Time for some muscles," he said and walked towards her.

Finally after three weeks of selling, cleaning, and moving their things into the house Darla had inherited in the quirky little desert town of Twentynine Palms,

Kevin returned to the almost empty shed and carried the box into the house. Whoever in Darla's family bought this gem probably did so before moving and homesteading here.

"Are you really going to work on that thing when there are all these other projects in this old house?" Darla's brown eyes were glaring at him.

"Yes, I am. This is an after hours project for fun. We've been working like dogs and you have your scrapbooking that you work on every evening."

"I'm recording the changes we're doing here. It's a record of our lives."

"Don't get snappish. You're still doing it for fun. This is my fun. Which would you rather it be: the Net or a couple of hours on this?"

Darla considered. When Kevin went on the Net, he could be gone until almost morning. "You're right. I'm being selfish. What should we do with that old shed? It's an eyesore."

"Maybe we could throw on a coat of paint and you could use it for your plants."

"No, I'm not going to mess with the yard. The plants there are fine."

"We'll do just like your grandparents then and dump all of our undone projects in there to thoroughly confuse our grandchildren."

"First you have to have children."

"Right," he muttered and retreated to the office/den combo they had created in the smallest bedroom. It was a never ending argument that usually ended with Darla's tearful, "When will you he be ready for children? When you grow up yourself?"

Kevin found himself working on the old radio for hours, sneaking off at every opportunity, frustration building as the radio would emit a squawk or two and fall silent. He finally went online and found old tubes at outrages prices, gulped, and paid. The arguments with Darla about his time cloistered in his den grew more heated. He would tear himself away for a day or two and then return determined to make this low tech item work.

Every night after her shower, Darla would stop by hoping to persuade him to return to their marital bed. Tonight she heard the hum from the radio and saw Kevin's face lit with eagerness.

"You did it!"

Kevin looked up and smiled. "Yes, I did it. It's working." He turned back to the machine and started turning the knobs again, his forehead wrinkled and his mouth pulled tight.

"What's the matter?"

He shook his head, twisted the dial, and removed the earplug. "I'm not sure. I think I may be receiving a foreign broadcast. It's difficult to make out anything when it's all so garbled. I haven't been able to understand a word. Maybe I should disassemble it again and really clean it. The dial isn't turning properly. I can't seem to pick up the right frequency. The tuner may need checking, and repositioning the antenna might bring it in clearer."

"Leave it for tonight, darling. You'll see it all in a different light when you step away from it for a while. You've been so involved with it." She eyed him anxiously.

Kevin shrugged and turned off the machine. "I was so sure this time. You're right. We both need a break."

He felt rejuvenated the next evening when he stepped into the office after dinner. Perhaps Darla was right. Sex could enhance one's attitude and brain. Kevin started by removing the dial and placing it back into position. He then adjusted the dial before inserting the earplug.

The voice was scratchy, but there was a voice: a male voice.

"I welcome this opportunity to talk with someone. It has been a very long time, Friend George."

"Sorry, I'm not George. I'm Kevin. George, if you mean George Kliner, passed away thirty years ago."

For a moment, silence reigned over the airways, and then Kevin heard a sigh. "That's sad news indeed, but I had not heard from George far longer than that. He complained about the coal fumes in the city and swore he would move. Did he do so?"

Kevin shook his head. How many years could it possibly be?

"Yes, he moved to the desert. How is it we are talking? I thought this was a regular radio, not a ham radio. There's no mike, no towering antennae. What's going on?"

A polite cough greeted him and then the scratchy disembodied voice began again. "There are many things I don't understand either. I can tell you that the 'radio' you have is possibly unique in your spiral."

"*Spiral*? What are you talking about, man? Who are you? Where are you?"

"My name is a variant of Gregory. It's rather difficult to pronounce in your language (English, isn't it?), but it means 'valiant watcher' in English. Why don't you just call me Greg? You are Kevin, correct?"

"Greg, just how can we be talking?"

A long sigh greeted this question and the voice became deeper, tinged with disappointment. "I had so hoped for a meeting of minds. Someone that would be content to discuss philosophies, but by the sound of your voice I can tell you are upset. I can't possibly explain the mathematics of the spirals. I'm much too ordinary. Perhaps another time when you are less agitated."

The radio went back to static and buzzing. Kevin twirled knobs and used the flat of his hand to hit the side like he had seen people do in the old films. Finally, he gave up and turned it off. He would return tomorrow night and use his computer. Forget mysterious voices from nowhere. It was a hoax of some kind.

The next night he sat at his screen answering personal e-mail and checking out the new videos, but his mind wasn't focused. His eye kept straying back to the silent radio. Would Greg still be there? Maybe he could learn more just by listening or hearing exactly what Greg wanted. What if Greg was right? What if by spirals he meant something like that new string theory he had seen on PBS when Darla insisted on watching it. It would be way cool if he, Kevin Alley, discovered a parallel universe. He'd be famous. First he'd need information and documentation. If he could get Greg back, he could set up a recording unit and have it all down. He rolled his chair over to the radio.

"Greg, Greg, are you there? Hey, dude, I didn't mean any disrespect. It was just overwhelming to hear your voice."

"Ah, Kevin, it's good to hear from you again. Tell me, where are you located?"

Warning bells went off in Kevin's head. Did this guy want information about the Marine base?

"I'm in Twentynine Palms, California," he said stiffly.

"Why that's the United States in North America. So the radio is still there and operational."

"What's it like where you are, Greg?"

"It's very boring most of the time. I watch and watch, but not too much happens. I really think our equipment needs to be upgraded. I don't suppose radios look much like that one anymore."

"Like, dude, radios can be as small as your thumbnail, but most are sleek and compact. We haven't used tubes for years. It's all about transistors, electronic boards, sound, micro chips and style."

"Fascinating. Have you managed to add viewing?"

"Your spiral doesn't have television? How do you pass your time?"

"By television, you mean a combination of radio with a screen for viewing the performance, don't you? If so, yes, I'm familiar with it."

"But, I don't understand. Radio is one media and television is another."

"That's there. It's not that way here. I told you things are different. The machines we have bridge the gap." Greg switched to another subject.

"Are you married, Kevin? George was I know. He and his wife had a little girl, about three-years-old, I believe. You said something about a wife. Perhaps you have children too."

"Yeah, I'm married to a real knockout, but no children. My wife, Darla, keeps harping on having a family. So far I've managed to avoid that trap. What about you, dude? Are you married with children?"

In response, Kevin heard a polite cough.

"No. Marriage isn't considered a necessity here. I believe there were children at one time, but things change."

"That's crazy. Don't you know what happened to your own children?"

"I didn't say they were mine. I said there were children at one time." His voice had become scratchy again. "I believe there's something I need to watch right now. Perhaps, I can arrange a system where we can see each other." The transmission went dead.

Greg was back the next evening. "I'm sorry, Kevin, I wasn't able to arrange a television type of transmission. It seems this might interact with some of the technology you now possess. Perhaps we can describe each other. I'm, oh, I'd say early middle-age with brown eyes, and a fairly straight nose."

Kevin shrugged. He had turned on his recording system before turning the radio on. It had been one long argument with Darla to convince her he needed it when she was talking about hardwood floors for the kitchen.

"Hey, that sounds like me, but my nose is a bit pointy on the end and I'm not quite forty. Why are your superiors so fearful of mingling our television systems?"

Greg's voice became throaty, husky, almost caressing. "It's better this way. The need to know is always there, and the imagination is more powerful than the eye. We can ignore whatever physical faults either of us possesses.

"George used to do a lot of reading, Kevin. Do you have that habit?"

"Naw, I'm more of a sports guy if I ever have leisure time. Reading is for technical manuals. I prefer working with electronics and the computer."

"A computer, my, my, your little corner of the universe has sped right along with its technology. Since you're accustomed to more advanced thinking, perhaps we can create a doorway between our spirals. Would that interest you? George and I had started one, but then his voice disappeared."

"Build a doorway to your spiral? How would that work? You mean you need a frame and a doorjamb?"

"Ah, not quite, however, Kevin, we will need a tonal frame. I'll gather my wits this evening and go over the mathematics. You do play a musical instrument, don't you? That was so common long ago."

"I've CDs and DVDs. Would that do?"

"How do you create music with them?"

"The music is encoded on them. I listen to them."

"No, no, that won't do. These musical tones must be in sequence at a certain pitch."

"How could music cause an opening between spirals?"

"As I explained, Kevin, it has to do with tonal pitch combined with a certain frequency on both sides. Harmonics, I believe it is called. I'll get back to you as soon as I have the answers."

Kevin sat for awhile. Was it time to bring somebody in on this? No, but if he had the doorway in place, they would have to believe him.

Darla would have a fit over buying musical instruments. He wheeled the chair over to his computer. He knew this might take days.

* * *

"Well, Kevin, I've the answer I was researching. It is possible to create the frame between our spirals. I hope my two day absence didn't disturb you."

"Why would it?" Kevin didn't mention taking his annoyance out on Darla or how she retaliated by not speaking to him.

"Are you familiar with wind instruments that one blows air into?"

"Sure, you mean like a trumpet or a sax?"

"My familiarity with your terms is less than adequate. Let me describe what I mean. It has a windbag with a pipe for blowing into, another pipe coming out of the bottom for fingering the melody, and then there will be three upright pipes. I believe these instruments are favored by a race called the Scotts. Can you procure one?"

For a moment Kevin was stunned. "Dude, are you serious. Those things screech, and I have no idea how to play one."

"Ah, but we need the tonal quality. You really won't need to play a tune. You'll just need to experiment and hit the right tone. I'll tell you when you do and then count out the timing."

"We'll see, but it's going to take some time, George. There's nothing like that around Twentynine Palms."

"Then why do you live there? Where George once lived they had the most modern selection of items."

"I agree, but the living costs elsewhere are horrendous. My wife inherited this house and certain, uh, financial securities. I can do most of my work from home on the computer and travel maybe once or twice a month. We're living the good life."

"How long would it take to procure this instrument? Do you have to travel far?"

"Greg, I can go on the computer right now and see what they cost and how long it takes to have one shipped here."

"Excellent, but before you do that can you tell me about the night skies? George explained how brilliantly the stars shone in your spiral. Perhaps a description of the constellations in your area would help me determine how much things have changed."

"Uh, like, uh, I haven't really noticed, but people claim stars are brighter here. I spend most of my time online at night."

"Online? What type of term is that?"

"It's like an electronic web for information, for trades, and for selling. It's how I conduct my business too."

"Ah, yes, your electronic connections. Quite interesting. I'll have to research the stars by other means. Tell me is your world still at peace and experiencing economic deprivation?"

Kevin stared at the radio before answering. "You must be referring to George's world. It's nothing like that now. There seems to be some kind of war going on some place at all times. Right now the most killing is being done in the Middle East and Africa. As for economic deprivation, that only affects those without a job. Even then the government pays them money. Of course, they can't afford the big screen TVs, but most of them have TVs. Right now it's worse than it should be, but it's improving."

"Really? What about the hobos? What happened to the army of men riding the rails looking for work?"

Kevin stared at the radio. "That was the depression. It has been over for years and we're coming out of a recession now. A lot of people came to California back then, and later others keep pouring in. Now they come for better jobs or to become famous in Hollywood."

"Did their places of origin become depopulated then?"

"Not exactly, Greg. The other places are overflowing with people too."

"I'd forgotten what a fecund group you are." Once again the dry chuckle came through the speaker.

"Now, Kevin, to create this doorway, we do need a wall devoid of the ability to see outside and one wall with a small viewing port, windows I believe you call them. It's to ensure the right resonance. If you have more than one of the windows that George described, you'll need to cover them. You must forgive my ignorance. It may have been those questions that upset George. I'm thinking of my work area, not yours."

"How do you watch if you can't see out? Are you using something like radar?"

"Ah, that comes as close as any explanation. Of course, that didn't exist in George's day. Interesting, but do you have the type of space we need?"

It was Kevin's turn to chuckle. "There's a window here, but it's larger than a viewing port. It's not large, about forty-eight inches wide and sixty-three inches long. I'm able to close the blinds. All the other walls around me are blank except for pictures and the closet doors which are closed. There's a minimal amount of furniture. Do I need to take down the pictures or move the furniture?"

"Perhaps, I'll do a few more calculations. Would you be able to wall up a portion of the window?"

"Not without causing a major disruption to the house or to our bank account. It's not something that would sit well with Darla."

"Ah, the same old story. Did you know that George's wife kept sending the child into his room to steal a radio part or break it? I think he finally gave up fighting with her. Well, I'll make those calculations and see what the possibilities are. In the meantime, you'll be able to procure the instrument."

The radio began the familiar squawking when Greg's voice vanished from the airway. Kevin shrugged. He had time to surf the net and see what was happening in the world and to find out how much a bagpipe cost. Darla finally managed to extract him at midnight, but he didn't mention the bagpipe.

He spent the next day arguing with himself about the cost of the bagpipe with his desire to complete the doorway. From the snippets Greg had let dropped it sounded like he, Kevin, might be able to give the world new technology. Fame, renown, money, it could all be his while he was still young enough to enjoy it.

After dinner he broached the subject to Darla.

"Are you crazy? Fifteen hundred dollars when I want new wood floors? You just bought that stupid sound system. There's no way! If you'd stopped spending money like we're in the same league as Bill Gates, we could afford children!" Darla stalked out of the house.

Kevin glared after her. That was her way: Voice a dramatic pronouncement and then go for a walk. It would do him no good to go after her, as she wouldn't be speaking to him. Instead he went into his office with his credit card before going to the site with the bagpipes. What he hadn't told Darla, was that fifteen hundred was probably the cheapest one. Rapidly he tapped in his order and checked the expedited shipping square. He would be home when it arrived, not Darla. Who wanted children or wood floors when an important discovery was within his reach?

* * *

"Kevin, are you there?"

"Yes, I was wondering how long your calculations were going to take. It's been over a week. I've had a fight with Darla every night over this. It looks like I'm going to be moving. We need to get this started if it's going to work. She won't let me have the radio. Technically, it is hers."

"That would present a real problem, however, won't it take longer to procure the bagpipe as you call it?"

"Greg, it arrived two days after we talked."

"Ah, I see. Your postal system has improved dramatically. Well, in that case, this should work well. My original figures were correct. I do tend to worry needlessly. Have you practiced with the bagpipe at all?"

"Once, and Darla came unglued."

"Your wife is glued together?"

"That's an idiom, a slang expression. She became angry and threatened to take an axe to the door and to the bagpipe. Will this take long?"

"Not once you hit the right note."

"That's a tall order. Right now Darla is at the store, but I'll lock the door."

Kevin hefted the bagpipe into place and proceeded to make the instrument squawk and protest. He kept moving his fingers on the bottom pipe, but he couldn't detect any sort of tone change. He lowered the instrument and realized he was panting.

"Did you recognize anything, Greg?"

"Yes, but you didn't hear me shouting. Try to match this tone."

Greg listened, but the tone sounded nothing like he'd ever heard. "I dunno, Greg, this is a long shot. Maybe some lessons would help."

"No, no, you're doing fine. Try again."

Kevin wasn't certain, but there seem to be a note of desperation in Greg's voice. He raised the pipe to his lips and commenced blowing. His attempts were ended by Darla banging on the door.

"Kevin, if you don't stop that noise, the neighbors or I will be calling the police. Are you insane?"

"Greg, there's an emergency here." He moved the dial to another station and admitted a very angry Darla.

"This has got to stop! If you must practice that thing take it away from civilization."

"I could sound proof this room."

"With what? You've spent all of your money and most of mine. For the first time since our marriage, I'm beginning to be glad we don't have children. Divorce is so much easier that way." She flounced out of the room.

Kevin turned the dial back to 101. "Greg, are you still there?"

"Yes, what happened?"

"Now Darla's threatening to call the police and divorce me."

"Perhaps, if you were to hear this tone again and practice away from people, you could replicate it within the next day or so. Try each hole on the pipe and listen to it."

The tone played again and seemed to burrow its way into Kevin's brain.

"Okay, Greg, I'll be back when I hit it."

"Don't take too long. I'm really anxious to be, ah, rather to know your space a little better."

"Anxious? Like is there any hurry on this?"

"Oh, no, no, not really, it's just impatience on my part." The tone droned out into the room again and the radio returned to its empty static.

After losing a day's worth of work, Kevin returned from the desert feeling invigorated by his walk and the time on the bagpipe. He was certain by next week he would be able to produce the tone. Then he'd connect with Greg while Darla was at a meeting of some church or women's group. Didn't modern day women eschew such things? If it weren't for all her money and this house, maybe a divorce wouldn't be such a bad idea.

The evening that Darla left for her meeting, Kevin waited until he saw her pull out of the driveway before contacting Greg. She was really nagging for children now.

"Why did you marry me? For my money?"

To Kevin, it was blackmail pure and simple. He turned the radio on.

"Greg, I think I've got it."

"Excellent."

"What happens when I play the three notes? Do you appear to me, or can we both see each other?"

"Oh, we'll see each other. Perhaps we can even, ahem, shake hands. That is what you do in your society, right?"

"Yes, do you have some other type of greeting?"

"Quite different, I assure you. Are you ready? Remember, three times and stop."

The tone came from Greg's side and Kevin raised the bagpipe, hitting the tone three times.

The frame appeared beside the radio, not on the wall. At first it was a milk-white opaque blob with wisps seeping into the room and dissipating. Gradually, it assumed the form of a rectangle, but instead of a scene of Greg seated by a radio or machine with visual capacity, Kevin saw Greg standing there with a smile on his face. The vision was startling. Greg looked like a mirror image of himself except he was wearing a smooth, bluish robe.

Greg's hands shot out, and he grasped Kevin by the arms. "This is wonderful." He twirled Kevin into and through the white blob and smashed the radio.

"There, that should make Darla happy. Thank you, Kevin, my friend. You can't hear me now, but I've plotted this for a very long time. It's your turn to be the Watcher for the Unknowns. Just think how happy your Darla will be to have a husband who wants children."

Greg found the bathroom, looked in the mirror and smiled. He ran a hand over his neatly combed, thinning, brown hair. Kevin, no, Kevin now Greg had been right, his new nose was rather pointy on the end, his eyes were brown, and the woman in the picture on the dresser was a real looker.

Kevin, now Greg, would be eligible for rotation in about a thousand years into a different spiral. He, the new Kevin, intended to put the smile back on Darla's face. After all, Kevin, now Greg, had said she wanted children. There was a satisfied smile on his face as he turned off the light and went into the living area to await Darla's return. Life was about to become bearable again.

The Kiss

She felt the two soft, childish lips, and they were soft, so soft against the side of her chin.

"Thank you, Mommy," came his whispered words.

Who is this man-child with the unruly thatch of dark, coarse hair, Mona wondered. My son is a grown man with children of his own, and she woke with the feel of the kiss gently lingering.

She swung her feet over the edge of the bed and waited before standing. Her thinking was fuzzy, her stomach beginning to tighten. A feeling of disquiet filled her being. She mentally shook her head and breathed deeply. I need a cup of coffee, she decided, but still the unease persisted. She was far too old too have another child, and Phil was dead, dead, dead. Nothing, nothing would bring him back.

She leaned against the door frame. "Please, God, don't let the tears and anger begin again." He was so young: only 58. He shouldn't be gone, and she shouldn't be alone. He was the strong one, but now he wasn't and she was. It was a battle she had been fighting over and over for a year. Her back straightened. First put the coffee on and fix breakfast.

Later that morning, she stood at the opened patio door looking out on the back lot. A dark head appeared over the fence. A young boy waved merrily at her.

"Hi, I saw that pretty tree all in bloom. What is it?

"It's a desert willow. It will bloom for months, and there's a wonderful spicy aroma when you're next to them."

"Wow! That's the prettiest desert tree I've seen. Can I smell them too?"

For a moment she hesitated, but her grandchildren were hundreds of miles away. This child looked about Mark's age.

"Of course you may if your parents say it's all right. I don't believe I've met them."

"I dunno." For a moment disappointment blanked his grey eyes. Then he cheered up. "I'll go ask if it's okay and be right back. Okay?" He smiled and disappeared.

Within minutes he returned ringing her doorbell.

She led him around to the back and through the gate. He sniffed at the flowers and a smile lit his face.

"Thank you. They're great." He smiled at her. "I gotta go now." With a wave of his hand, he ran off.

What a strange child thought Mona as she returned to the silent house, but then in its own way the desert is a place that draws strange people.

She had retired with her husband into this economically depressed area. They were able to buy the house for an incredibly low amount. Within less than two years, Phil fell, and in one week's time had passed away. The diagnosis: Extra Dura Hemorrhage. Translation: A ruptured blood vessel causing blood between the brain and the skull. If she had let them operate, it would have increased the bleeding. The chance of survival was twenty percent and he would be brain-impaired, bed ridden with a feeding tube. Phil had always been adamant when he had been able to discuss such an event.

"No needless operations or heroic medical procedures to prolong my life. I don't want to live like a vegetable."

There was no operation, and he was gone. She returned to the lonely house, too exhausted to consider moving, and the thought of facing the stress of working again was not an economic necessity.

One week after the awakening kiss, she awoke feeling groggy despite sleeping for eight hours. Bright sunlight fought against the bedroom drapes holding the day away. She pulled on her robe and slippers. A cup of coffee would fortify her for the day's meaningless chores. As she approached the kitchen, she wondered if she could force herself to eat this morning. Suddenly her mouth was open and she was gasping in air. The child sitting at the kitchen table smiled, his grey eyes lighting up at the sight of her.

"Where is your mother?"

"She went away. She said I should come with her, but I didn't want to go yet."

The Kiss

She swallowed. "Who looks after you?"

"Oh, some very nice people, but they come and then they go too. Now you can be my Mommy and some day you'll take me with you." He smiled again, his grey eyes alive with trust. "I'm hungry. Can you fix me some eggs and toast?"

She blinked her eyes and for some reason her appetite returned. Not only her appetite, but her zest for the bright, sun filled day. Within minutes the frying pan sizzled and she cracked the first egg.

Over breakfast they began to laugh and talk.

"Do you like school?"

"We're learning divisions and fractions. Fractions are easy. I like them better than percents, but they're easy too."

"Is your teacher nice?"

"I like her because sometimes she says we need to go out and play."

What a strange school. Mona had much to dwell on when he left with a cheery good bye. I should have probed deeper, she thought, and quickly called after him.

"Will someone be there to take care of you?"

But he was gone, running through the backyard to some place beyond.

Her days went better as an outward semblance of happiness settled around her. While she worried about the child, she did not actively seek him out.

Two months later he was back.

"Look how you've grown!" Instead of eight, he looked to be about ten.

Once again he favored her with a smile full of joy at seeing her. "They say it happens. Do you have a snack?"

This time they talked about pets. "Do you have a dog?"

"I did once, but it's hard to remember. They say that memories are like fog, full of misty things."

All too soon it was time for him to go. He said someone was calling him, but she heard nothing.

Her days took on a false normality of volunteering and keeping the house. The pain of that red-hot iron claw ripping at her empty insides she could mask with a bland face and a false smile. The boy was soon forgotten except in those odd moments when she remembered the feel of his lips on her chin.

She so completely forgot the boy that she was shocked when she found him in her kitchen one late afternoon when returning from the museum. Her stomach contracted when she realized he had aged again. How could this be?

This was a pimply teenager with a nose too large for his face and feet that tripped over each other. He looked like pictures of Phil when Phil was fifteen-years-old. This man-child could have been theirs.

He laughed and lunged forward to give her a joyful hug. "Thank you for not kicking me out before. I really needed someone to talk with. Do you have something to eat? Something like a sandwich?"

"There's tuna fish salad in the fridge."

This time he started the conversation as she assembled the sandwich to stop her hands from shaking.

"You're not really my mother, you know."

"I know, but you seemed to be so trusting. It would have been difficult to go into all the reasons that you could not be my son."

He devoured the sandwich, smiled at her, and ran out of the door.

She realized then that she had never asked his name. How puzzling, but it all seemed so natural.

Six months later he returned. She had just entered the kitchen to brew the coffee when he turned from the window and held out his arms.

Mona could not move. It was Phil. Her Phil of the grey eyes and wide shoulders, smiling at her, his eyes alive with admiration and desire, and he was young, so very young: a man in his prime. She was old. Gravity was winning and there was grey at her temples. Her hands showed the years far more than her face, but no one would ever mistake her for being thirty again.

Suddenly he was beside her and his arms swept around her drawing her close as he hugged her.

"I've missed you so much," she heard him murmur as he seemed to draw in the smell of her.

It's strange, thought Mona, I can smell his smell.

"Phil this can't be."

"But it is, darling. I've come back for you. Come with me now."

"I can't. You're dead." A sob started in her throat.

He tipped her head up and she could see his smile.

"Phil, you're young again and I am old. We cannot be together."

"Yes, we can. The other doesn't matter. You are still you."

"No, Phil, look at me. I'm alive. This can't be. Oh, my darling, whatever this is, it is wrong. You must go."

"You can walk with me to the door, can't you?" He bent his head and gently kissed her cheek.

His arm was around her waist and she was walking with him just as they did so many times before. They seemed to float through the door into the sweet spring desert air.

Bath Time

It's nice sitting here on Grandma's lap with Cissy. There's room for just the two of us. Before she just held Jarrod and never held us anymore.

Grandma is holding us tight and telling us how beautiful and brave we are. She wants us to say a prayer for Jarrod's soul and ask the angels to guide him. Great lumps of water are running down her cheeks and making funny, pink squiggly lines. Cissy keeps wiggling so I take her hands and help her fold them.

"My brave, beautiful, little girls," Grandma sobs again. "To think you're only five." She was hugging me extra tight.

We could hear sirens coming and Mama ran to the door. She is still carrying Jarrod, all wrapped up in that awful, blue blanket he always chewed on. Only now his skin looks all white and blue.

All sorts of people start running in the door with funny looking boxes with tubes and dials and hoses. It's just like on TV.

"Come, girls," Grandma says and drags us toward the bedroom.

"I wanna stay!" That just sorta popped out, but I do want to know if Jarrod has really, really gone away.

"I just put him in the tub with the girls." Mama's words are high and all screechy. Just six inches of water. That's all I ever use."

They've put a strange thing on his face and are pumping his chest up and down. Mama keeps on screeching.

"Ashley (that's me) is so good about watching them. I just needed their clothes. Oh God! Why didn't I take him with me? Why did I leave them?"

"How long were you gone?" The woman in uniform asks in the same tone Mama uses when she is trying to distract us.

"Oh, I don't know. Just a couple of minutes to get their clothes. Then I answered the door when my mother knocked. Oh, please, please, help my son." Her voice was a wail.

She is screaming, but not Jarrod. He'll never scream again. I can tell by the look on their faces. Now Mama and Daddy will be like they were before Jarrod came. That's why I had Jarrod pretend to swim. I even helped him. I held his face under the water so he wouldn't be afraid.

A Victim of Murder

Edith Longley walked the eight blocks from the convenience store to her home in Twentynine Palms. Rivulets of water ran down her temples and her hair was damp. She'd worn a three-quarter length sleeve blouse to hide the bruises on her arms. Ed had shaken her this morning when he discovered the fridge did not contain his favorite beer.

"The oleanders need trimming. There'd better be a cold beer in there in one hour."

Edith had quickly dressed and ran to the store. After forty-seven years of marriage to Ed, she was unable to defy him, but then she never had. She'd meant to be up earlier, but had stayed up late to watch the show on television. Edith loved the quiet house when Ed was gone carousing and the television was hers. She could watch all the crime shows she wanted. If she had learned to read faster, she could have read more crime books by authors like Ann Rule, but instead of school, she helped her folks pick cotton in the Oklahoma fields. When they brought in machines, the folks had moved to the city.

At the store, Edith ignored the pain in her arm when she took the beer from the cooler. As always, her graying brown hair was done in a bun at the nape of her neck. Ed wouldn't let her cut her hair short even in the desert summer heat. She smiled at the clerk and handed her the six pack of beer. It was another new clerk, not really young, but her long, brown hair was tied back and she was chewing gum. She smiled at Edith and quickly slurped out the meaningless words, "How are you today?"

Edith responded as always. "Good," her brown eyes betraying no emotion. As the clerk rang up the sale, Edith placed the money on the counter.

Ed had given her the money this morning. He knew to the penny how much change there would be and Edith counted it before placing the coins into her purse. She used her good hand and arm to pick up the plastic beer-filled sack and hurried out the door.

This summer had been much hotter and more humid than last year. It was beginning to remind her of Oklahoma and the cotton fields she worked in as a child. At least Ed let her run the air conditioning. He didn't want to come home to a "hot box."

The eight blocks let her mind wander back to last night's true crime show about a woman that poisoned her husband with the sap from oleanders. She would have gotten away with it if the man's brother hadn't kept complaining to the police that his brother didn't have a bad heart. He kept at them until they exhumed the body and did an autopsy. Edith vaguely remembered hearing something similar in one of the newscasts, but it seemed to her that the state did an autopsy automatically because the man died at home. Of course, that wouldn't have been a very long show.

As Edith neared home, she could feel the perspiration running into her eyes and she quickened her steps. The almost teenage girl, Kylie, from down the street was running toward her carrying her black and white cat named Cookie.

"I'm telling my Mom that your man kicked my cat. He's a monster." Her black hair bounced around her ears and her pink, smooth face was flushed. Her mouth was pursed and the brown eyes looked as though asking, "How could anyone be so mean?"

"I'm sorry, dear," Edith managed to say as Kylie ran by her. Both knew that Kylie's mom would do nothing. She was a single mother and worked "down the hill" in Palm Desert. She left home early in the morning and arrived back late in the early evening.

Edith choked back her emotions. There hadn't been time to ask Kylie if Cookie were all right. The first time Kylie brought Cookie by she had been a nameless fluff-ball.

"Why that kitty looks just like the coloring of the cookies you buy in the store."

Kylie had been delighted and christened the kitty Cookie. "And you can be like a grandmother," she assured Edith.

Edith had taken to leaving tidbits of food outside for Cookie whenever she saw the cat or Kylie. She'd hold the growing kitten and croon to it. Cookie made up for the pet Ed wouldn't let her have. Now it was doubtful if she would see Cookie again.

Ed wore his long-sleeved work shirt to keep from getting scratched or cut by the oleander leaves. Dust and leaves stuck to the sweat-drenched garment. His hair had receded a couple of inches, but his eyes were still that deep, unexpected blue. For a man that drank too much and had to take heart medication, he sure didn't look like it. His face wasn't nearly as wrinkled as hers. Edith kept hoping that the liquor and the medicine would kill him, or at least make him sick. So much for hope, she thought bitterly.

"Gimmie one of those beers," he ordered.

Edith quickly extracted one and handed it to him.

"It might have warmed up some."

"It's still better than water." Ed pulled back the tab and drank. "I had to chase the neighbor's cat out of here. It was leaving a mess under my oleanders." He scowled at the shaded spot beneath the bushes. "They better learn to keep that cat indoors."

Edith left him working at bagging the rest of the leaves and branches. He'd be all morning cleaning up the results of trimming his prized oleanders and taking the trash to the dump. Then he wouldn't be back until later for a nap and dinner before going out again. Edith couldn't understand why Ed loved oleanders. She thought they were dirty, messy, dusty, and the flowers much too small. It didn't matter as Ed thought they were beautiful. He raved about the new hybrids with different colors and how much bigger and prolific they were. Edith knew they were ugly and dirty, and now she knew they were poisonous too. How she longed to take a knife or shovel to them.

Walking into her cool, kitchen soothed Edith's sour outlook. This was the nicest home she'd ever lived in. Even being married to Ed was worthwhile as long as they lived here. She had enough scars and healed ribs to prove how much she had paid for it. At least Ed let her watch TV as long as the house was clean and his meals cooked and ready for him when he returned home. She would just keep slicing him up into little pieces in her mind before she went to sleep.

Of course, Ed could return anytime since he retired. Sometimes it wouldn't be until after one a.m. when the bars closed, but he still might want his hot meal and it better not be a TV dinner. She stuck the beer in the fridge to cool and walked into the master bath to wash off.

She looked in the mirror. Her grey hair and the wrinkles creeping up both sides of her bony face told her she'd never find another man at her age. The nights might get lonely while Ed partied with his buddies, but they were peaceful when he was boozing and the television was hers. Not like when Ed was home and she couldn't touch the remote.

Edith shuddered at the thought of the shacks her folks rented before they left the cotton fields in 1957. The city had more opportunities like her new school her parents insisted. For Edith the school was huge, scary, and way over her head. Her classmates laughed at the easy reader she'd been assigned. Her humiliation was complete when they put her in a room filled with Spanish speaking Mexicans and blacks from Mississippi and Arkansas. There was only one other white female in the classroom. Finally, she quit when she was a sophomore. It was easier to sling hash. That's where she'd met Ed in San Diego. He swaggered in and sat at the counter where she was working.

"Hey, brown eyes, how about a cup of joe for a returning Marine, and maybe something else on the side."

When she put the coffee and creamer in front of him, he started to laugh.

"Sugar, you're a girl after my own heart. I forgot there are decent women like you left in the world."

His blue eyes, uniform, and steady pay were enough to turn any young girl's head. He asked her for date before he left. Before his new orders came through, they were married.

She expected to be hit occasionally. After all, that's how her parents lived. Ed's life wasn't any different. He had grown up in the cotton fields of Texas. It wasn't until she started watching all those TV shows that she realized that hitting wasn't normal. Try as she might, she couldn't figure out a way to live without his income. They couldn't even figure out how to pay the mortgage when he retired.

Then one of Ed's old Marine buddies had written about how cheap the houses were here. They'd made a trip two years ago and the houses were as low priced as the man had claimed. Ed went home and sold their place immediately. On a return trip, he paid cash for this two bedroom home with built-in cabinets, fancy wooden vanities with marble countertops in the bathroom, real carpet in the living room and in the bedrooms. There were big closets and nice tile in the kitchen and the two bathrooms. They had enough money left to rent an apartment until Ed retired. Ed might be nicer if he just quit drinking, but then Ed was mean whether he drank or not: just like the rest of his family.

She heard talking out in the yard. Strange, Ed rarely talked with the neighbors. Then she heard his truck start up and leave. She breathed a sigh of relief and walked down the hall towards the living room. She was just in time to answer the doorbell.

Dolly, Ed's fifty-five-year-old baby sister, stood there beaming at her, peroxide hair frizzled and split at the ends, her blue eyes darting right and left as though to assure herself that no one had seen her come here. As usual Dolly was wearing a mishmash of clothing: a stained, sleeveless purple tank top that encased her midsection like a sausage and knee length turquoise stretch pants that strained against the heavy thighs and waist.

"Well, are you going to let me in before one of them grandkids track me down? Ed said there was beer in the fridge." Dolly leaned her beefy weight against the door and pushed. The force sent Edith backward.

Edith felt her stomach tightened as she led the way to the kitchen. If she gave Dolly any beer, Ed would take out his revenge on her. If she didn't give Dolly a beer, Dolly would go crying to Ed and he would still beat her for not being nice to his baby sister. Reluctantly, she set the beer out for Dolly. Edith had hoped to get away from Ed's family when he retired, but the San Bernardino County DHS had sent Dolly's daughter and her three kids up here to live because it was so much "cheaper" than San Bernardino. They said Ashley could make the welfare check last all month. Hah, thought Edith, not when you drink it down and smoke it. Edith didn't know what Ashley smoked, but whatever it was, it cost money. The kids never had new clothes, but wore things the Shepherd's Closet handed out. Dolly always explained how she came along to help with the children. Dolly then ignored the children except to defend their bad behavior. There were times when Edith felt Dolly was spying on her to report to Ed.

Dolly took a long swig. "I needed that. The landlord was over raising a ruckus about the cooler and the stove. He claims the kids damaged the oven door by jumping on it and one of the kids must have shut off the cooler without shutting off the water. He wanted them to pay for a new stove, any roof repair, and this huge water bill. He lies. How does he know? He wasn't even there, and he certainly can't prove the kids did anything wrong with the swamp cooler or the stove. If he didn't have such cheap junky appliances in his apartments, they'd hold up better." She took another drink. "Now he's claiming we have to move if there's one more complaint from anybody about noise."

Tears filled her baby blue eyes and the mascara on the bottom eyelids began to descend with the tears. "It's just not fair that everybody picks on the kids the way they do. They're good kids. Just high spirited." Dolly was rapidly diminishing the can's contents.

Good kids, my foot, thought Edith. They're nothing but hellions and hoodlums. She pitied their teachers and their landlord.

Dolly didn't notice Edith's silence and kept right on talking. "I told Ashley to quit paying the man and save her money for a deposit on a new place. He can't just put us out. 'Course it might be difficult to find a place without references." Dolly drank more beer and smiled at Edith. "That's part of why I came. You and Ed can either write us out a reference that we were staying here until we had money for an apartment, or we'll move in with you."

Edith's heart lurched. At least it was quiet here when Ed was away. That was usually all day and most of the night. He would be home to watch sports events or work in the yard, but most of the sports events he watched in the bars. Then she realized that Ed wouldn't allow kids or their cat around.

"I'm sure Ed will write the note for you."

Dolly swigged down the last of the beer. "Thanks, how about joining me in another one?"

"No, I have to have those for Ed when he comes home."

Dolly snorted, but stood up. "Well, I gotta go. You should join me over at Stumps sometime." She went out swinging her wide hips like some man was going to make eyes at an over-age frump. Edith knew better. Men quit looking at older women once they realized you were over forty or fifty. A glaze would come over their eyes and they would shift their focus to search for younger prey. At least that's the way Ed's friends had been whenever he brought them home. Of course, that didn't happen very often as Ed could be jealous, and that ended a friendship real quick. She took her purse and headed for the door. She had to replace that can of beer before Ed got home.

When she returned, Ed's pickup was parked in the driveway and Kylie was walking down the street towards the neighbors.

"Is your kitty all right?"

"Yes, he's all right, but I'm never going to let him out again, and I'll never come near your place again." Kylie kept walking.

Edith felt a stab of loneliness. Kylie had all sorts of tales about school and the park with its swimming pool and the people that went there. Ed wouldn't take her to the park, and it was too far to walk. She had hoped that some neighbor would offer to take her, but the neighbors always seemed to be gone or busy with their own lives. Edith had lost track of her family after Mama died. Ed didn't want her to associate with them. He always found something nasty to say.

She walked into the cool house and found Ed sitting at the table talking on the telephone.

"We can meet there about six. It'll start to cool by then." He was still for a minute.

"Okay, pal, talk to you later. The old woman just walked in. She better have my other beer."

He's been in the fridge already, thought Edith.

"Dolly was here for a visit. I couldn't be unfriendly."

"You didn't have to offer her a beer."

"I didn't. She just took it." Edith saw the frown and the blue eyes narrow. Quickly she held up the other can.

"I went and bought you another one."

"Where'd you get the money?" Ed was starting to get up, his right fist doubled.

"They had your brand on sale this week. It didn't cost what it usually does." Edith was surprised at how rapidly she thought up that lie and quickly changed the subject.

"Dolly wants you to write a reference for her saying she and Ashley and the children have been living with us. The owner's going to kick them out of the apartment they're in now because the kids broke the oven." What was wrong with Ed? Usually he wasn't drunk in the morning, but ever since he started that new heart medicine, he'd been acting differently. He'd get drunk sooner and that meant he was mean all the time.

"Why does Dolly stay with that bunch of losers?"

"Well, it is her daughter and grandchildren."

"We oughta invite Dolly to move in here. We've got that extra bedroom and she can give you a hand with the work." He nodded his head like it was settled.

Edith felt panic building and her heart began to flutter. Dolly had never done an honest day's work in her life. If she wasn't in the bars, she was watching soap operas. Dolly would never let her watch her shows again. Please, God, she thought, let Ed forget about that before he sees Dolly.

"Maybe I should call her right now." Ed punched in the numbers and she heard the ringing on the other end.

"Hi, Doll Baby." Ed used their family nickname; one that Edith thought obscene.

"I hear your gonna need a place to flop. We've got that extra bedroom and you're welcome to it."

"No, that doesn't include Ashley and her kids. There ain't room for them or that damned cat. It's you and you only."

Ed was silent. Edith could hear Dolly, but she couldn't make out the words.

"Okay, Doll Baby, we'll expect you next month then."

He hung up the telephone with satisfaction. "She'll be moving in at the end of the month when their rent is up. It seems Ashley's found some boyfriend that will put up with the kids. If not, they may go back to the city in a couple of months. Good riddance. It'll be great having Doll Baby around, right, Babe?"

Ed stood. It wasn't right. He was still six-foot tall and muscular. He had a bit of a beer gut, but with all the booze he'd put away over the years, he should be shriveled or bloated like a dead pig left in the sun. Even his blond hair had changed to silver. The nurses at the doctor's office always fussed over him. The only consequences of all that drinking seemed to be high blood pressure and too much cholesterol.

Ed stretched and yawned. "I'm going to take a nap, Babe. Tonight I'm meeting Pete and Dave at the bowling alley. Have to rest up for the big match."

Edith knew better than to turn the TV on if he turned it off or to change the channel. She went outside, but even in the shade of the oleanders towering over the front porch, the heat was too much to bear. She went back inside, mixed some ice tea, and picked up a magazine with fancy room pictures she'd bought at the Friends of the Library sale. She'd read it four times, because Ed had thrown away the rest. She had just saved enough for the next sale when today she had to replace that beer. Her mind could not stay with the words. The horror of living with two Longleys was more than her system could tolerate. She had to do something before Dolly moved in.

At four o'clock she began fixing the evening meal. She could hear Ed moving in the other part of the house and taking a shower. He came back in the kitchen just before five and looked at the tuna casserole and peas.

"I ain't eating that garbage. I'll pickup something at the China Inn. At least that man can cook." He slammed out the kitchen door. Edith looked at the casserole. It would take her a week to eat all of that. She'd have to clean the refrigerator tomorrow and throw away what had set there too long. Ed never took her to the China Inn or the How Chow, but then she didn't like Chinese food. He did, especially the hot and sour soup. He complained that they weren't like the Chinese restaurants in LA, but he continued to eat there. He had taken her to the China Inn for their anniversary, but not to 29 Palms Inn Restaurant or Denny's where they served real food. She fixed her plate and turned the television to "her" channel.

She planned on being in bed by the time he returned. If she were in bed and asleep, Ed usually didn't bother to wake her up and start an argument. He would be too drunk.

Five hours later she turned out the light and slipped into bed. She heard the garage door and closed her eyes. Edith had long ago learned how to pretend sleep. When they were young it didn't matter, Ed would do what he wanted whether she were asleep or awake. Sixty-eight was another matter. He would stumble in and mutter at her, take off his pants and shirt, and go to bed. He'd take them off, that is, if he weren't too drunk to unbutton the shirt. She'd almost fallen asleep when Ed came stomping into the bedroom.

Edith made no movement other than breathing, but it didn't matter. His belt came slashing down across her arm and she moaned. Ed grabbed her shoulder and flipped her over, the belt slapping down against her hip and legs. Then he stopped. Did he consider it enough? Who knew what went through his mind.

Ed wasn't anywhere around when she woke up, but he must have remembered that he drank the beer. There was money for a six pack lying on the table with a note: Babe, pick up my beer. At least he'd made coffee. She'd have breakfast before she left for the store.

As she walked out the drive, she noticed the sap left on the cement from the oleander bushes. Perhaps the oleanders did have a purpose in her life. Edith wondered whether the sap came from the leaves or the branches. She snapped off a leaf. There was no sap. Oleander leavers were like the leaves of trees or other shrubs. The sap was in the branches and the sap was poisonous, and Ed wouldn't even know he'd eaten it.

A trip to the library would mean a walk up a hill to the light, down the hill, and partway up another hill before her destination. There had to be books

A Victim of Murder

there that would tell her how to make hot and sour soup. She could keep that on hand to heat up for Ed when he came home at night. She wouldn't have to eat it. She didn't like Chinese food. Edith returned to the house for a sheet of paper and a pencil.

She was panting when she arrived at the library to find the doors locked until 10:00 a.m. By the time they opened and helped her find a book on Chinese cooking precious minutes were gone. She was almost frantic by the time she found the recipe and copied it down. What would Ed do to her if he came home and found her gone?

The day's walk was worse than yesterday. Edith nearly collapsed from the heat before arriving home. She really wanted a shower, but there wasn't time. As soon as she put the beer in the fridge, Ed drove in the garage. She quickly pulled out the lunch meats, mayo, and mustard for his sandwich.

"Where's my beer?" Ed didn't really look at her. He just pulled open the door and grabbed one. "What's for lunch?"

"Sandwiches since it's so hot."

Ed didn't say anything. He just went into the room with the TV. He knew she would carry everything to him. She also knew he would want her to eat in there with him. Like a trained servant, she carried in the trays and carefully set them down.

"Do anything today?" Ed always liked her to report on how much work she had done. It was like he checked to make sure she didn't go anywhere.

"I went to the library."

"What for?" Ed's teeth closed with quick precision on his sandwich. His method of eating reminded Edith of a snapping turtle, but she didn't dare laugh at him.

"I thought I'd look up some Chinese recipes so I could learn to make the food you like so much."

"That would be great, Babe. Now let me watch the news." The last was a growl more than speech.

Lunch passed in silence until he stood. "I think I'll take a nap before showering. Oh, I saw Dolly today. She was hunting boxes for the move here."

Edith's face froze, but her mouth said, "That's nice," and her heart started that fluttering again. She quickly took a swallow of water and almost choked.

Ed laughed. "If you make real Chinese food, I'll eat it." Still chuckling he went to bed.

Edith went into the kitchen and read the recipe from the library. She then took out paper to start her grocery list. She certainly didn't keep straw mushrooms, white pepper, tofu, and several other necessary items in her kitchen. How could people eat those things? Worse, she couldn't get to a real grocery store for two more days when Ed took her. At least he would let her pick out the things to make him something special, but that didn't give her much time. Dolly would be here in one more week.

Dolly dropped by the next day when Ed was ready to leave for his evening out. "Ashley says she needs another four weeks before she can move in with her boyfriend. But he fixed it so the landlord can't kick us out for another four weeks. It seems the landlord has to give us a written thirty days notice. Just his say-so ain't good enough. I'll stay and help Ashley with the kids. That way she can save more money."

"Doll Baby, you need to think about yourself."

"I am, big brother. I couldn't live with myself if I didn't do all I could for my baby girl."

"Suit yourself. I'm heading toward the Break 'n Run."

"Why don't I hitch a ride?" Dolly waggled her finger at him. "You just have to promise not to drive off my gentlemen suitors."

They were still laughing they climbed into Ed's pickup.

Edith heaved a big sigh as they drove out. She didn't care that they hadn't wished her goodbye or invited her along. Dolly wouldn't be here for four more weeks. Maybe never.

After their shopping trip, Edith assembled the ingredients for the hot and sour soup. Sweat covered her forehead when it came to the last part about pouring in the beaten eggs without stirring until they rose to the top. Finally the egg portion floated on top. Gingerly, she stirred and then tasted it. Was it too salty? Next time she wouldn't add salt until the last. The recipe said to add the mushrooms and chopped green onions and then heat and serve. She turned off the burner, went into the garage and took the small rose cutter. She snipped off a tender oleander branch from an out-of-the-way spot and carried it into the house. There she let the sap drip into the soup. She had no idea how much sap it would take and didn't dare taste the soup. She didn't want to die.

After an hour of cooling she opened the can of straw mushrooms and put those and the onion in the soup. Then she poured the soup into a bowl, put a lid on it, and placed it in the fridge. She would heat that up for Ed when he came in. Otherwise she could serve it to him for lunch. She disposed of the oleander branch and washed her hands. Edith slept well that night.

Ed didn't show up until the next morning looking pale. He took a shower and went to bed. When he got up he claimed to feel well, but Edith simpered over him. "I think you should call Dr. Robertson. I'll just throw out this hot and sour soup. It can't be good for you if you're not well."

"I ain't going to no doctor. Let's see if you learned to fix decent food."

Edith put the heated dish in front of him.

Ed dipped his spoon in like it might poison him, and slowly sipped it. "Ain't bad," he admitted. "Something tastes a little different. Too much salt. Leave the stuff out. Doc says I'm to lay off it anyway."

Edith cleared the dishes and stacked them in the dishwasher while Ed went to watch television. She took her book and went in after his second bellow.

She read, but didn't really read, and waited. Nothing happened; nothing that is, except when the news was over Ed left without saying where he was going. Then Edith remembered the show. It had taken more than one dose of the doctored food to kill the man. At least she'd bought enough fixings for another batch, but she'd have to wait a few days before serving Ed that again. Today was Tuesday so maybe Thursday or Friday would work.

Ed came home early that night looking pale. Instead of changing the TV station or ranting at her, he went directly to bed.

The next morning, Edith waited for him to tell her never to make the soup again while he sipped his coffee and nibbled at his food.

"Is something wrong?" Edith's voice was timid.

"Naw, too much excitement last night. I had the winning shot lined up when some dude started a fight. I ruined my shot and the police came and closed the place down. My heart took off like a trip hammer."

"Maybe I'd better call the doctor."

"Don't touch that phone. I'm fine now. I'll be back when I feel like it."

Edith waited until he was out of the driveway and called the doctor's office to report Ed wasn't feeling well and that maybe his medication should be changed.

"I'll need to make an appointment." The receptionist was adamant. "Nothing can change unless Ed comes in for a check up."

"All right, I'll see if I can convince Mr. Longley." Edith smiled to herself as she hung up. She knew there was no convincing Ed.

On Thursday, Dolly dropped by just as Edith threw the oleander branch and leaves into the garbage.

"You've been cutting on Ed's oleanders?" It was more of an accusation than question.

"Oh, my, no, that was just something he missed in his rush to get to the dump." Edith congratulated herself. She was getting as good at lying as any Longley.

Dolly snorted. "Now you're even cleaning outside. You are a real neat freak. Is Ed at home?"

Edith wanted to scream you know he isn't and you just came by to sponge another beer, but instead she smiled without gritting her teeth. "No, he left over thirty minutes ago. If you go to The Bowladium, you'll find him."

"Naw, I ain't the bowling type. I get my exercise elsewhere." One heavily mascara lashed lid winked at her. "Gotta beer?"

Inside, Dolly wrinkled her nose. "What stinks in here?"

Edith quickly set the beer on the table. "That's all I have. I have to save the rest for Ed."

"What's that smell?" Dolly wouldn't let go of the notion.

"Just something I made for Ed."

"He ain't going to eat that!"

"It's Chinese food. He likes it. I got the recipe from the library."

It was time to change the conversation. "Anyway, Dolly, I'm glad you dropped by." It really wasn't a lie. "Ed came home the other day looking just awful and I couldn't get him to go to the doctor. He wouldn't even call. I thought maybe you could get him to go to the doctor."

"Why would I do that? Doctors just take your money. Then they send a fax to the drugstore and it costs you more money."

Edith couldn't figure out why Dolly was complaining. After all, California and the federal government paid her medical bills. Somehow Dolly had convinced a doctor in San Bernardino that she couldn't work. Dolly was on disability and Ashley collected all sorts of money from the state for the kids. At least Ed had a job all his working years, and she would get his social security and most of his pension when he died. She could live on that.

Dolly took a swig of beer. "Why don't you show me the bedroom that I'll have?"

Edith could think of lots of reasons she not show it, but obediently led the way back. "It's the spare room. Right now there's things stored in the closet that we'll have to find a place for."

Dolly carried her can with her. One step into the room and she stopped. "It's painted blue. That's creepy. It needs to be something like red or purple. I'll have Ed fix that when I move in. What's the closet like?"

Edith felt the rush of blood to her face and kept her back to Dolly. Awful, horrible colors. She couldn't let this woman into her house. Ed might just paint that room red for his baby sister.

"Maybe Ed can get it painted for me before I move in. We're going to stay where we are until we have to move. Ashley's friend is going up north in a couple weeks and doesn't want kids in his home unless he's there. I bet he turns into a real jerk."

After Dolly left, Edith almost tasted the soup from force of habit. Hurriedly, she emptied the teaspoon into the sink and turned on the water and garbage disposal. She stared at the disappearing contents for a long while and then quickly shut off the disposal and water. That was how she could get rid of the soup. She could barely contain her excitement.

At dinner that night, Ed tried the soup. "Not bad, Babe, but it's just a tad too bitter. It could use more salt too."

"Well, you know what the doctor said about salt."

"Don't tell me what to do, and don't leave out my salt again."

Edith decided it must be fairly good because Ed ate three bowls of it before leaving. She debated on whether to dispose of the last bowl or wait to see if he died. If he didn't die tonight, he might eat more of it.

Edith could not focus on the television program. She kept going to the kitchen and looking into the refrigerator. Then she would look out the window to see if Ed or a police car was out there. Finally at ten o'clock she went to bed.

Sometime during the night Ed stumbled in. He was too drunk to take off all his clothes and fell onto the bed without removing his shoes. If Edith hadn't moved he would have pinned her down. She retreated to the spare bedroom for the rest of the night. Next time she'd put in more oleander sap. Maybe she should leave out some of the vinegar. From the smell of the sap, it had to be bitter.

Ed was up before she was, and had changed clothes. She noticed there was vomit on his shirt tossed at the laundry basket. When she walked into the kitchen, he was eating the last of the soup.

"Just make it right next time, Babe."

"Okay, Ed, I will."

"Doll Baby wants me to paint that room purple or red."

Edith bit her tongue. She knew better than to protest. Ed would really paint it one of those colors then.

"And she wants me to put down new pink carpet so it will be glamorous." He pushed back from the table. "Well are you going to stand there and gawk or are you going to make me some coffee and a decent breakfast."

Edith swallowed and opened the pantry door to pull out the coffee. "Carpet's kind of expensive," she ventured. "And it might not go with red walls." Inwardly, she wanted to run into her bedroom and cry.

"You women! You don't really think I'm going to make it look like some trashy dive, do you?" He snorted. "Did you put Doll Baby up to that?"

"No, Ed, you know I don't like red—all that much." It was best not to let Ed know she didn't like the idea of it on the wall at all. Dolly wears red all the time."

"No, she don't."

Edith bit her lip and began fixing his oatmeal. "Are you feeling better this morning?"

"What was wrong with how I felt last night?"

"Well, you were a little peaked yesterday."

Ed snorted. "I'm going to watch TV. Bring me my breakfast when it's ready."

Edith heaved a sigh of relief. She'd make that soup again next week. Before she could take the eggs out of the fridge, she heard Ed in the bathroom being sick. She quickly ran water in the empty soup bowl. Then she went to the bathroom.

Ed was bracing himself by holding onto the tank cover. Edith couldn't believe how sick he was.

"I think I should call the doctor."

Ed straightened like he was going to hit her, but quickly bent over the stool again before he slipped to his knees, and continued to heave whatever was left in his system.

"Call Walt," he commanded. "He can take me in. No need for an appointment. They can see how sick I am."

Edith didn't object. The longer Ed stayed away from a hospital the more apt he was to die. She dialed Walt's number, but there was no answer. She left a message.

She went back to the bathroom and found Ed still on his knees, holding on to the lid. He'd stopped heaving, but his skin looked pale and his forehead was covered with sweat.

"He didn't answer. Let me call the ambulance, Ed."

"No, call Tops."

Edith considered. The taxi was probably cheaper than the ambulance, but she doubted if they would take him once they saw how sick he was.

She went to the telephone and called. This time Ed was on the floor when she returned. Edith went back to the telephone and called 911. Then she recalled Tops and cancelled. Next she went back to the bathroom and made sure the toilet was flushed and brought Ed a pillow. His breathing was ragged and he looked awful.

The ambulance arrived in less than seven minutes. They asked about his doctor, took his insurance information, gave him oxygen, and bundled him on the gurney.

Walt called back and offered to take her to the hospital once he heard what had happened. She accepted as she could not drive. When they arrived, they found out that Ed had died in the emergency room. The report said "cardiac arrest caused by erratic heartbeat." The doctor confirmed that Ed was on heart medication and refused to follow orders when it came to drinking and smoking. There was no hint of an autopsy.

Edith was worn out with attending to funeral arrangements, arranging a service at a local church, and the funeral itself. Then she had ride the bus to the Social Security Office in Yucca Valley. She'd gone to the Reach Out office in the Senior Center and they helped her with all sorts of things. There was even an insurance policy that Ed had bought years ago. Social Services helped with details about titles on the pickup truck and promised to help her when the death certificates came in. With the insurance money and by selling his truck, she could buy a little car and hire someone to teach her to drive again. Until then, she would rely on Reach Out and the little market not too far away. The days were getting cooler too. Edith found herself singing for the first time in years.

When Dolly offered to move in right away, Edith gasped. "No, no, I want to be alone."

Edith began to let the answering machine take all of her calls. She never, ever called Dolly back. She began keeping her doors closed and locked. Edith wanted Dolly to be far, far away. *She'll go away if I don't let her in* kept running through her mind.

Dolly would come by and bang at the door every week. Edith would ignore that also. Her walks to the market in the morning were quite pleasant. After school started, Kylie would walk with her chatting away like the old days. Edith was practically dancing when she returned home.

She walked in her house and set the groceries on the counter and took a big drink of water before turning to lock the door. Dolly was standing in the doorway, swaying back-and-forth and smiling.

"I came over to talk about moving in." Somebody had curled her hair into ringlets and it looked foolish framing her wrinkled face like a schoolgirl's. Dolly swished her wide body over to the table and sat down.

"I don't suppose you got a beer handy, do you?"

Edith rejoiced. This was her home, not Ed's. "No, I never buy it anymore."

Dolly shrugged. "Some ice water would be good, and lots of ice." She smirked at Edith. "I came over to tell you I'm moving in tomorrow."

"No, this is my home, and I'll call the law if you try that. It would be trespassing."

"Go ahead, and I'll tell them how you were messing with the oleanders and used that for the Chinese food." Dolly's blue eyes were hard. "I watched that show too. I didn't put two and two together until I remembered seeing you at the oleanders the second time. You took the stuff inside. Now get me that ice water and the telephone. I'm going to call a painter. I've never lived in a house this nice."

Edith numbly walked to the counter for the glass. This would be worse than living with Ed. How could it happen? This was her beautiful home. She had everything planned, and she heard her breath draw in like a sob, but it was rage: Rage at her own impotence.

"And don't start that bawling on me. I'll knock some sense into you if you don't hurry up." Dolly swung one beefy fist and struck her on the back. "Ed told me how to make you behave."

Edith straightened and reached for the upper cabinet door with her left hand. Her right hand opened the drawer. She pulled out her carving knife. With her left she slammed the upper door and whirled, the knife descending time after time.

Edith never remembered Dolly screaming, but somebody must have heard her. The police were there before Edith could cut Dolly up and dispose of her.

Ghost Town Remodel

Kimberly Walker parked her pickup on the wind-blown debris laden desert street and surveyed the worn buildings lining the road through a once prosperous town. The weathered, store fronts were empty and any lower level windows were long ago broken or boarded up. Several of the brick and the wood buildings had weathered the neglect to remain in decent shape and some were two stories tall. One, she suspected, had been a bordello rather than a hotel.

The handsome building survived as a business for the surrounding area long after the mining town faded away. This had been one of the last of the gold mining towns and people still lived here when the electrical lines went through. Everything would need to be rewired, but she could be connected to the grid or go solar. The architect's plans for her new home, workshop, and store were safely bundled in her cabinet in her travel trailer.

For a moment something white seemed to flutter in the upper window. Probably the wind blowing paper through an opposite window Kim decided. She took her clipboard, held her hat firmly on her brown hair, and walked up the steps of the suspected bordello, and pushed the door open. Dust and spider webs covered the front counter and the key box behind it. The first time she'd visited here she had rubbed the dust away from the counter in a circular patch. Rich mahogany tones glowed in the sunlight and she knew she had found her home. It had taken two years to purchase the properties she wanted and have the architectural plans drawn and preliminary estimates given.

This time she meant to properly inventory every room. The movers would be here in the morning to transfer the items she selected to the workshop, and then load up the rest for disposal.

The plumbing, electrical, and carpenter contractors were due in two days to begin their reconstruction. There was, she reflected, something bizarre about a dot.com millionaire buying part of a desert ghost town from Riverside County and planning to live and work here.

Kim surveyed the lobby, a large area that would be revamped into a foyer and living room. The smoky, glass mirror by the stair reflected a blurred image of a slim woman with blurred brown eyes, and designer jeans. Nothing in the image betrayed her forty-five years.

The stairs were in decent shape and she ignored the dust. The spider webs, however, clung to her. A broom would have been handy. She walked every room, marveling at the furnishings: a bed in one, chamber pot in another, a dresser or chair, a dressing table with chair, a chest and mirror, lamps, and tables. Cleaning and zeal would give her coming enterprise an inexpensive inventory.

Night was approaching when Kim finished her list and the desert wind became severe. Dust obscured the road. It was one of the things she been warned about. The back of her canopy covered pickup held food and water, her bedroll, and camp cot. Her laptop and personal items were in the cab. She could sleep here and not bother driving back to town. She wouldn't need to rise early to be here before the movers. After they finished, she would drive into town to retrieve her travel trailer.

Fighting the force of the wind, Kim carried everything into the hotel. She unfolded the cot and placed it against the far wall on the lower floor of the hotel entrance. Her rolled out sleeping bag went on top of the cot. Beside it she placed a small table she'd found in one of the rooms. Her red wind-and-go lantern on the table added a spark of color.

"Who are you? What are you doing down here? Madame Bella will be furious if you aren't in your room. Only I have permission to be out."

Kim whirled around. The husky voice came from the bottom of the stairs. A woman dressed in a long white, lacy dress stood there. Her blond hair was swept up into a bun, her face covered in too white a powder, and her lipstick was a garish red. In her gloved hand was a small white, crocheted evening bag.

"This is where I'm sleeping. Who are you? No one lives here anymore."

The woman gave a sneering smile. "You may not think this is living, but it's quite comfortable. Whoever you are, you aren't welcomed. I'm sure suitable quarters can be found elsewhere."

She glided through the front area, her feet completely hidden by the gown. Before opening the door, she turned to Kim.

"Get out of those men's clothes. You're a disgrace!"

The woman turned back to the door. "Oh, there's my gentleman caller now." She opened the door to the last vestiges of light.

"Hello, Mr. Mellon, it's such a pleasure to see you again." The door closed behind her.

Kim hadn't seen anyone at the door. She ran to the door and pushed it open against the wind. The woman had experienced no such problem. Kim stepped out far enough to look up and down the street. The woman was on the inner side of the sidewalk flanking the main road, her left arm lifted as though entwined in a man's arm. At the end of the street, she turned and disappeared from view.

How strange, thought Kim. That she had just witnessed a ghostly visitation did not enter her mind. Logic was her tool at work and ghosts were not logical; therefore, ghosts do not exist. Someone was playing a sick, practical joke or the woman was completely delusional and perhaps dangerous. Should she leave? There was a dust storm out there and night had settled quickly. Kim could barely see across the street. It would be best, she thought, to wait it out.

She used a can of Sterno to heat her canned stew and some of the water for a cup of green tea. The wind kept banging things outside, making a repeated knocking noise against the door and front. Kim ignored the noise and the howling wind by working on the laptop. Two hours later, she decided to turn in. Tomorrow, the laptop would need a charge once she had her generator hooked up. At first sleep was difficult with the wind banging loose boards, the noise of creaking buildings, and the wind's tonal effects. Gradually she sank deeper into a sound sleep.

The slamming door woke Kim as the morning sun pushed against the darkness creating a soft light. Kim would have preferred going outside to watch those spectacular colors that would soon cover the sky and gild the surrounding mountains in rose-gold light, but one look was enough to see the woman was injured. Her hair was no longer in a neat bun, but spilled down her back. Her right sleeve was pulled away from the shoulder seam and a rent over six inches long was in the skirt portion.

"Are you all right?"

The woman spun and a horrible blackness had spread beneath one eye. Her bottom lip was puffed to twice the size of what it had been, the red lipstick mixed with red blood.

"Why are you still here?" The woman screeched at her.

"I own this building now." Kim was exasperated with the silly creature, but still she looked like she needed assistance.

"Do you need a cold compress? I still have water and ice in my cooler. It might take the swelling down."

The woman's one good eye glared at her. "No, I want nothing from the likes of a freak like you that wears men's clothing. This was just a bit of a misadventure, and you have no right to be here. You'd best leave before Madame sees you." The woman turned and fled up the stairs.

Oh, fine, thought Kim, by the time I chase after her, she will have disappeared down the back stairs. She gave a mental shrug. It was time for breakfast and she needed to at least run a comb through her hair before the movers arrived. She also needed to check with the local police when she went into Blythe to see if anyone was living out here.

The movers drove up in a one-ton truck at eight o'clock. The man that stepped out of the drivers side wore washed out denims and a light blue cotton shirt.

"Miss Ambrose, it's good to see you again. Which building did you want us to start on?"

Kim found herself admiring his muscular arms and wide shoulders. *He must be over six feet*, she thought as she needed to look up at him. His smile set well in that tanned skin and showed much better in the bright sun than in his small office.

"Hello, Mr. Williams. The front counter and key box, plus all the furniture needs to come out of the hotel right in front of us and moved to the "workshop." It was a loose term, but the building she had chosen as her work site was made of brick and its tin roof intact. "That will be the third building to the west. If there is anything in the building to the left of this one, you will need to clear that also as that is where the store will be."

"No, problem. Hey, Marc, we'll start at the top floor and carry things out."

He turned back to her. "By the way, boss lady, my name is Curt."

Kim decided she liked his blue eyes and brown, wavy hair as much as she liked his smile. She put out her hand to shake his.

"I'm Kim, and I'll help carry the smaller items. First I need to show you where I want things placed so I can get at them for restoration."

Four hours later, they grinned at each other. The furnishings had been moved to the workshop in one trip. The men had loaded the heavy things on the truck first and then the smaller items.

Curt offered his hand. "You were a real help, boss lady. I'm sorry this is the only time we'll meet. I'd like to see what you are going to do with all the furnishings. That iron bed looked like it needed to have the rust sandblasted off."

Kim never let opportunity pass. "Who do you know that has a sandblaster?"

Curt's smile was back. "That would be me. Just moving things wouldn't keep me working. I'm also a general handyman."

"In that case, why don't you let me spring for lunch in town and we'll discuss how much you charge for sandblasting. That is, if you don't mind dining with someone who looks like she's been physically working all morning."

"You look great to me. Follow me and I'll drop Marc off and we'll eat at Rosa's. It doesn't look like much on the outside, but she makes a mean gyro with garlic sauce."

"Sounds good."

He was already at the entrance when Kim walked up to Rosa's restaurant door.

Curt opened the door with a mock half-bow. "Welcome to my home away from home."

Lunch was better than she anticipated. While eating they discovered they both cared deeply about history and enjoyed restoring artifacts from the past. "I'll also need some help with setting up the display cabinets and doing the larger pieces once the construction is underway. Do you think you could work that into your schedule?"

"I'd enjoy it. I charge twenty dollars an hour."

"Fair enough on the carpentry work, but I'll need a better grasp of the restoration needed. We'll discuss that later."

"It's a deal. I'll do the iron bed for two hundred dollars."

"Agreed."

She and Curt exchanged cell phone numbers before she made her final arrangements for moving out to the site. She was anxious to return and didn't bother finding a police station. It was late when Kim headed back to her town as she thought of it. That only three of the buildings were hers mattered little.

It was her home. She would be on site during the rehabilitation to prevent any loose ends.

* * *

"Hey, lady, did you know you had a resident ghost or two?"

The question was posed by Nelson, the superintendent over-seeing the construction work.

"There are no such beings as ghosts."

"Yeah, well, you'd have a hard time convincing two of my workers. One almost quit. Some dude in a black suit threatened him when he was hauling in drywall. When he put down the drywall to challenge the guy, he disappeared. The other one is my woman hardware installer. The blonde ghost upstairs threatened to have her thrown out if she didn't leave her "boudoir." That one disappeared when Sallie went after her with the drill running. Later somebody pulled Sallie's hair, but backed off in a hurry when Sallie swung the drill around."

"Maybe it's squatters."

"No, Ms. Ambrose, I'd say you have two bona fide ghosts running around here. Lots of these old mining towns do. You could make a fortune off of it. Maybe you could even have a taped TV show. It would sure give this place a lot of publicity."

"Don't be silly. Ghosts are for Halloween, nothing else. As for that woman, I have seen her, but she is real."

"You saw her? Where? When?"

"The first night I was here and spent the night in the building. I haven't seen her since. I assumed she left when she saw that I was living here."

"Ma'am, ghosts don't leave. Just be careful she doesn't do more than pull hair. Excuse me, Ben is waving me over, and we have a schedule to keep."

Sallie quit that night, and the person taking her place was male. During the three months it took to complete her home, two more men reported seeing the dark-suited, belligerent male. The man, however, would disappear as rapidly as the woman.

Kim worked on her restoration of the furnishings from the hotel seven hours a day and spent time putting lamp kits into the kerosene lamps for her new home. She knew this was a good move as there had been six sales over the summer without any advertising. People driving through stopped to look and found her discoveries delightful. Soon she would put an ad in the regional papers, set up her website and connect it with an online auction site.

If everything went correctly, the building inspector would be here at the end of next week. The painters were due to be here tomorrow.

She walked briskly over to her "new" business. Curt was putting the finishing touches on the front display cabinets. Kim liked his dedication to keeping the structures true to their original nature.

"I wonder what purpose this building served," she ventured. "I like to think of it as place to eat. Maybe if I investigate underneath, I'll find some old china."

"You're more apt to find bottles. It was probably a tavern for the miners to stagger in and out of." Curt grinned at her.

"At least these two rooms give you plenty of space. If you're successful, you'll be able to expand. Maybe someone likes old liquor bottles."

She smiled back. "Do you always think the lowest of people?"

"No, but there's still more profit in booze than in eats. Besides, a lot of the mining companies hired their own cook to supply meals. It kept the men at the job and indebted to them."

She liked that in him as she hadn't expected a craftsman to know about history. Perhaps it was her perception of the world. People in small towns didn't always jibe with the evaluation of urban people.

Curt stepped back and looked at the display cabinets. "How does it look, boss lady? If you approve I'll get to work on the counters. That backroom might look better with some partial partitions to separate certain display items."

"I'll think about it. First I need to know if the county inspector clears my house for occupancy. If I need to expend more money, the answer is no for now."

"Fair enough. The inspector is due next Friday, correct?"

"Yes."

"It will pass. Would you like to have dinner at Rosa's to celebrate? My treat. Maybe we could even do some line dancing afterward. You've been camping out here too long."

"It's a date."

"We'll go into town in my truck and I'll bring you back just like a real suitor."

That Friday morning the sunrise threw rose colored and golden lights against the sky. Then the rose color swept over the surrounding mountains turning a beige world into one bathed in color. Kim washed her face while looking out at the mountains and marveled at the beauty that could suddenly envelope this corner of her new world. As she stepped out she saw the woman in white staggering to the front door. Her white dress was as tattered as before.

"Hey, you, stay out of there!"

The woman either didn't hear her shout or ignored it. She pushed on the door and entered the house.

How could she? Did I forget to lock the front door? The thought raced through Kim's mind as she sprinted for the door. The new lock was installed, but not locked.

Kim felt her heart racing as she ran into the foyer. The woman was nowhere in sight. There was nothing on the floor to indicate that anyone had passed through here. Kim looked at the stairs and ran up them waiting to hear the sound of a closing door. Nothing.

A thorough search of each room revealed the same thing: nothing. Where had the woman gone? There were no secret panels and new drywall and wainscot had been installed during construction. She hurried downstairs and checked behind every door and into every nook; all futile. Finally she gave up and returned to the travel trailer for breakfast and the wait for the county building inspector.

Curt picked her up promptly at 5:30 p.m.

"You look great, Kim." His blue eyes were smiling at her. "Today must have turned out like I predicted."

"Well, yes and no."

"Do you mean you didn't get the C of O?"

"Oh, yes, I have that."

Curt picked her up in a hug and swung her around. "I told you this would be a night to celebrate. Come on, let's go eat. I'm famished. I didn't have time for anything more than a sandwich today." He set her down, opened the truck door, and bowed.

"My lady, your chariot awaits."

Laughter drove away lingering worries about the disappearing woman entering her house into the background of her mind. Kim stepped up into the pickup.

Curt slammed the door and hurried to the other side, started the truck, put it into gear, turned on his country music, and headed towards town.

"After dinner, there's a band at the Corner Tavern. They aren't famous, but they don't go off key and the beat is great. The bartender makes a great mixed drink if you're partial to them." He began singing the words of the radio music and smiling at her.

Kim didn't want to spoil this time and said nothing about the woman until they were at the Corner Tavern relaxing over a drink while the band took a break.

"You've seen her how many times?"

"This makes the third time."

"And she disappears into nothing every time?"

"She doesn't vaporize," Kim snapped, sorry that she brought up the subject. "She's not a ghost. There aren't any such emanations."

"Have you ever seen her so-called suitor?"

"No, only the workmen saw him. Is she mad? Where is she hiding? And how does she get in and out of my house so rapidly?"

"Okay, I'll tell you what. I'll spend the night there," he paused to leer at her and elevate his eyebrows. "And tomorrow, Marc and I will move your furniture in, but tonight is for celebrating. We've both been working hard."

They laughed and danced until the place closed at two a.m. Then they went to an all night restaurant and had coffee before heading back to Kim's place. It was almost dawn when they pulled up in front of Kim's trailer and daylight was just tipping the edge of the world grey.

As they stepped out of the pickup, they saw a man and woman fighting in front of Kim's house. The tall, thin, dark-suited man kept slapping and punching the screaming woman. Somehow, she broke away, tripped, and fell to the ground. The man jumped on her and continued to punch at her face, tearing her dress as she tried to turn.

"Stop it. Leave her alone." Kim and Curt were both shouting as they ran to the couple.

The man stood and the woman scrambled to her feet.

"Who are you to interfere?"

"I own this place."

The man sneered at her and glanced at the woman holding her torn dress.

"Bitch," he howled as he jumped at Kim.

Curt pushed in between them and the man released his grip and went for Curt's neck.

Kim faced the woman. "Please, come inside with me. That man is no good for you."

"Who do you think you are?" The woman's hands encircled Kim's throat.

Time suspended for Kim and Curt as the other two dissolved into them. The four bodies became two.

A male and female were left looking at each other. The female had Kim's features, and the man had Curt's, but their emotions were their own.

"We're real again! That means you can marry me. Mrs. Mellon needs to go away."

"I will not marry you and you are to stay away from my wife and children. You viperous bitch!" He slapped her again as he spoke. "Promise me, no more demands or I'll have Madame toss you into the streets like the two-bit whore you are."

For a response, the woman reached down and pulled a pistol from her embroidered purse. The man jumped her again, shoving her arm upward, sending the ghostly bullet into the sky. He twisted her arm and threw the pistol a few feet away. He slugged her in the eye so hard she fell to the ground.

Both continued screaming curses at each other as the man pulled a knife from his boot sheath. Emily scrabbled towards her gun. The man brought his knife slashing downward, but Emily had grabbed her pistol and rolled to the side. His downward slash left a gash on her dress. The woman had held onto her pistol and shot one more time as the man's knife hand was raised for another blow. The man crumbled downward.

Curt and Kim were left standing in the middle of the street, hugging each other and swaying back and forth.

"Curt, what happened? I could never shoot anyone. How could I feel the blows? The ground? Hear the swish of the knife? Are you alright?"

Curt hugged tighter. "I don't know what happened. They, they were inside of us, but their ghostly weapons couldn't harm us. We can never interfere again if those two start fighting. They've been killing each other over and over again for over a century. Are you okay? Are you going to be able to stay here?"

"I'm still shaking, but this is my life. All my finances are tied up in this venture. They can't drive me away!

"My God, where is she going?"

Emily had rolled over. She was crawling towards the steps. She struggled up on her knees, stood, and tried to open the locked door. It wouldn't budge and she made the motions of someone opening a door and floated through.

"The inside is safe," she sobbed to herself. Emily smoothed her white dress, sniffed and went up the stairs. That hadn't gone like she planned, but Mr. Mellon would call for her again.

Mr. Mellon was standing in the street brushing the dust off his black suit. He adjusted his hat and went back down the street in the opposite direction.

Curt and Kim watched Mr. Mellon walk away. He disappeared from sight at the end of the building.

Between

It started with the noise of a hard, cracking sound. Its power shook the house, rattled the dishes in the cabinet, and caused a power outage. It was eleven o'clock in the morning and most were at work. This is Southern California and tremors have to be severe before most notice. Those that heard it assumed it was an earthquake or a horrible accident. Some ran out of their houses, but could discover nothing amiss.

I tried calling my power company, but my line was dead. I knew other people were calling the power company to find out how long the outage would be. My cell phone was useless and I had no land line. I went to my auto and turned over the motor to hear the radio. There were no stations coming in whether it was AM or FM except one local AM station.

A man's voice sounded like this was an emergency. "Please follow these instructions. We'll bring you the latest updates as soon as we make contact with someone. Right now, no one is certain what has happened. We cannot reach the governor's office. There are no casualties reported other than heart attacks and a few scattered accidents when the traffic lights went out. The mayor is recommending you turn off all non-essential appliances being run by electricity from generators as we do not know how long the fuel will last. All transmission lines are down. I repeat. Turn off all electrical appliances and lights. The hospitals have generators and are open for emergencies. Keep checking back to this station with battery power if you have batteries. Stay tuned for more developments." The station went dead.

Curious. I turned it off and stepped outside. Nothing seemed amiss. The street was still there; the lawns, the trees, and the skyline of downtown Palm Springs.

One elderly man was out on the street. Now he was gesturing at the blue sky; his companion, a dog was switching its tail back and forth.

I walked over to the next block to see if Vance had any ideas. He works at web designing from his home. Before I was at the door he came outside with a perplexed frown.

"What's going on? Anybody have any ideas?"

"Not really, unless you think this is a reality show like that old Twilight Zone program when all the neighbors get edgy because only one can start their car." Vance paused and asked. "You want to chance it and start yours?"

"I already did that for the radio. Next it will be when I head out for work."

"Mike, you'd better call first."

Vance always had to have the last word. I waved at him and returned home, shaved, and went to the garage. My car started, and I didn't hear any creepy music as I backed out, but the garage doors wouldn't close. Without electricity, the inside mechanism would not respond to the remote. I went back in and locked the kitchen door and reentered the auto.

The noon heat was verging on one hundred, but it was clear. Instead of the DVD I usually played, I flipped on the radio. It was strange. My satellite stations were gone.

"Now I'm ready for eerie music." I found myself speaking aloud and flipped the radio off. It was time to concentrate on driving the crowded arterial street. For some reason there were fewer people when I merged on to the I-10 heading west. I almost made it to Banning when the autos started piling up and a trooper was frantically trying to direct those that could to turn around and go back. I quickly pulled off onto the shoulder. What is going on?

The trooper walked up, disgust in his voice. "Mister, you can't park here. Go back while you can."

"What's the problem?"

"The road is gone. Now get out of here before I arrest you. You have my permission to drive across the meridian."

The number of cars was rapidly swelling, horns were honking, and people ahead of me were shouting. Since there were no cars coming from the west, I quickly drove across the meridian, and parked on that side. The trooper was busy directing everybody back. I got out of the car and ran forward. I looked to the south and the north and realized the landscape had changed. There were mountains in the distance, but these mountains had no vegetation and they were stark, bony-rock masses of black. I looked to the side and where there should have been vegetation and pavement there was desert; beige sand glinting in the midday sunlight. There was desert back behind me, but here? People had planted and cultivated crops; trees had been planted generations ago and they were gone. The skyline of Banning was gone.

I saw the trooper glaring at me and I ran back to my car. There was nothing to do but drive back to Palm Springs. I pulled out my cell phone and dialed work. Nothing, no sound, no robo voice telling me all circuits are busy, please try again later, just nothing. This was beyond bizarre. Where the hell was Banning?

Once I was back in Palm Springs, I pulled into a gas station. All the pumps had signs on them: Cash Only. Pay First.

I pulled up into the space in front of the mini-market and dashed inside.

"What's going on? How many people do you think carry cash?"

The dark-haired, dark-eyed cashier eyed me gloomily. "All the ATMs are down. So are our credit card systems. We're running on generators. No cash, no gas, or anything else."

I stared at her. "What does your home office say?"

"We can't connect with anyone. Look, mister, you want gas or not?"

I did a hasty calculation of the dollars in my wallet. There was barely enough to buy one meal out.

Another man walked in. "What the hell's going on around here? The phones aren't working; ATMs or credit purchases aren't working. How's a man suppose to get to work?"

The cashier plastered a tight smile on her face. "From what I heard, the job might not be there."

He stared at her and then glared at me. "Where's a bank around here?"

"About two miles straight down, but without electricity, it might have closed."

The man stomped out and another irate person took his place. They had helped me make a decision. I headed for my own bank. Surely, they had money for their depositors.

The bank, like many buildings in southern California, is a pink beige box with a column or two by the portal. The ATM had about a dozen disappointed people milling around, the drive-in-lane was full and people were lined up by the door. I obediently took my place and prayed it wouldn't get violent. People were not in a good mood.

"Is there anybody in there?"

"I don't know. I can't see through the other door."

"Hey, don't shove."

"Watch it, dude."

Several police cars, sirens blaring pulled up to the back. Someone sent their kid to check on what was happening (probably under the delusion that an officer wouldn't shoot a child). The kid came running back.

"They said everybody has to leave."

The police marched up and one officer stepped forward.

"Folks we need this area cleared. We had an alarm from here. A dangerous person may be in there."

A woman behind the door used a large key. Her face was sickly looking underneath that professional hairdo and business suit.

"Thank you for coming, officer. My name is Karen Overton. There's no robbery, but the alarm was the only way we could call you. Someone's locked in the Safety Deposit room and we can't get it open without electricity. Our generator isn't starting. We can't be open without electronics and I'm afraid all these people will be as angry as the ones inside. We won't be able to secure these doors without electronics either."

The officer's face had changed from annoyed to concern to stern to amazement with each of her sentences. "Okay, Ms. Overton, I'll send a man over to a locksmith's. Maybe he can think of a solution, and I can post two men until you get your generator up and running."

"But we need money. The damn ATMs aren't working," a man's voice yelled out.

The woman looked at him. "Sir, we've already dispersed the money we had available. We can't get to anymore."

The lights inside the bank blinked and turned on showing that the generator had started.

"Does the ATM works now?" Another voice yelled out.

"No, sir, just the inside will have funds.

"Officer, thank you for coming, but how do I get in touch with you when we run out of money again?"

He looked at her. "Lady, I don't know how you contact us. We don't know what's going on. We're spread thin with all the traffic accidents. You start to run low, just close it down. And don't let anyone else into that Safety Deposit

Room until the regular lights are back. You're lucky I don't write you up for a false report." He motioned the rest and they returned to their cars and took off, sirens and lights blazing.

We were permitted to enter five at a time. An hour later, I walked out with $500.00. It was the maximum a person could withdraw and when their available funds were gone the doors would be locked. I wanted as far away from there as possible.

Buying gas for my car was the next thing to do and then groceries and maybe some water. Otherwise everything would be gone—if any of those stores were open.

I finally made it home by four p.m. The neighborhood seemed quiet and I rolled into the garage and carried my purchases inside, turned on the radio.

The announcer was back on with these reassuring words uttered in a fast, clipped manner. "Everybody remain calm. For some reason, the landscape out there has changed. There has been no communications with any of the rest of the United States or elsewhere. If there is an emergency, contact the local police or sheriff's office. 911 may not work. A command center is being set up at City Hall. Remember, another update thirty minutes from now. In the meantime, stay way from Palm Canyon Road. There have been three bad accidents."

Once again there was dead air and I flipped it off. To console myself, I grabbed some food out of the fridge and made a sandwich on the theory that I might as well eat it before it goes bad.

While I ate, I wondered what it looked like from up in the air. I pulled out my cell and used the speed dial to call a friend that had a small plane when I realized that it was useless. I'd just have to drive to his place and see if he was there. I drove out to his home with a private air strip. This is Palms Spring, you know.

I could see Brett sitting in his office drinking from a can of pop. He had the door propped open for the breeze since air conditioning was unavailable. The thought of a summer here without electricity is enough to panic grown men. I knocked at the jamb.

"Brett, it's Mike here."

"I can see that." He looked up and gave a half-hearted smile. "Out wasting gas?"

"Yeah, well, I tried driving to Banning. Everything's changed, dude. Have you been up in the air?"

"No, I'm thinking and conserving my fuel."

"Why? If you don't use it, the police are apt to confiscate it."

:"That's true, but so far, I'm not making any noise. If I go up, everyone will see me."

"Has anyone been up?"

"If the reporters or police have, they aren't saying much. Why did you come over?'

I recounted what I had seen while Mike listened intently. When I finished, he crushed the pop can and stood.

"Thanks, Mike. That confirms my thinking. It's what I was afraid someone would tell me, but I'm glad you're here. I can use your help."

"Sure, what can I do?"

"Help me by going up with me and turning on these two DVDs players. I was trying to figure out how I was going to do that by myself. The plane is rigged for plugging them in. I have it for when I take up paying customers and they need to plug in for whatever reason."

"No problem, but why are you taking them up in the plane now?"

"Harmonics, Mike, harmonics."

"Huh?"

"Harmonics have been around for a long time. Did you ever take advanced math or philosophy?"

"That would depend upon your definition of advanced."

Brett chuckled. "It started with the phrase 'music of the spheres.' That would be Pythagoras with his ratios based on music. Then during the renaissance, the theory really became the properties of the greatest men in science when they searched for harmonies or harmony of the universe, if you will. It included people like Newton. The twenty-first century has brought us to the brink of cosmic harmonies. Mike, the harmony just got disrupted."

Brett hunched forward again to look down at his charts. "Something disrupted the tonal harmony. Somehow we need to be back in tune. I'm not a musician, although, I'm not sure this needs a musician. I think by duplicating their music, we'll be able to restore it. I've worked it out with certain formulas. I had started wondering about it last year."

"Brett, I didn't know you were capable of that type math."

"I can to a certain extent, but do you know what you can do with computers now? I hooked two of mine together and let them work at night."

"Here's another question, Brett. Why didn't the entire world crack up?"

"Maybe it did, but I'm hoping it's just this section of it. From what you've told me and what the news has said, we are in a different time frame. We need to go back or forward in time. That's something else that needs to be resolved. It's as though time and space actually warped from the discord."

"So how do you know what tones caused it?" I tried to keep sarcasm out of my speech and hoped he'd take it as skepticism.

"I was listening to the same music as they were playing at the Coachella Music Festival. According to the announcer two bands were playing the same song at once on different stages. I've used my generators to burn another copy of what I have. We're going up and play both at once. I'm hoping being up in the air, and having the sound turned way up will make up for the difference of not having amplifiers. If I'm right it should put everything back. It'll be a big help if you can push in both play buttons at once. I've already turned the sound as high as it will go."

"So how does it get to the outside if we and the DVD players are inside?"

"Another detail I took care of earlier. I've attached speakers to the outside and run the audio cords back inside to connect to the players. I used layers of duct tape around the windows where the cord is treaded through."

"It should hold." He muttered after a pause. He probably saw disbelief on my face.

"It'll be all right, Mike." Brettt grinned at me. "At least I think it will."

"What will be all right?"

He shrugged. "I'm hoping everything will be." He picked up the DVD players. "Shall we go?"

I'm not sure why I agreed to it, but what could be worse than the situation we were facing? There isn't enough land to support people with food. This is the desert and nobody but a few had gardens. People driving through on I-10 were trapped here. They'd be angry once the full perception of what happened hit them. Hell, they were probably angry already. I thought of that mob of visitors at the festival's center. That's thousands of people that don't live here.

Light planes aren't my favorite. The flooring between you and the outside world always feels insubstantial to me—like if I tromped hard on the floor it would break through and we'd be doomed. Following Brettt's instructions to use both the seat belt and the strap across the shoulder and chest didn't improve my worries. I pushed them out of my mind as Brettt soared toward Indio. The airport in Palms Springs kept trying to contact him for a flight plan and to warn him. Brettt ignored the radio.

As he neared the festival grounds he went higher into the thinning air.

"Get ready, Mike. Push them both when I say now."

We could barely see the edge of the RV park and then we were over the staging area.

:"NOW!"

I pushed both buttons. We both could hear that music; it was faint, but we could hear it. Brettt kept circling the area until we could not hear any sound from outside. I looked down.

"They've played, Brettt. Do you want an encore?"

"Sure, why not? Then I'll have to head for home."

The plane suddenly did a pitch and roll and then threw us side to side, rolled again while it seemed to vibrate. The vibrations were making my immobile body shake. Brettt was hanging onto the wheel and trying to bring the plane back under control. Then it felt like something turned it upright and Brettt managed to bring the plane around and head back towards Palms Springs. I wondered if my face was as white as his.

He flipped his radio back on as he flew over his field and banked. The landing was fairly smooth considering the beating we had taken.

I didn't leap out of the seat once we were down. First I had to unbuckle everything. I wasn't even sure I could stand. My legs were shaky and I'm pretty sure I was gasping for breath. Brettt opened his door and I opened mine before stumbling out. I was elated to be on desert sand again. It took several deep breaths for me to have sense enough to grab the DVD players and close the door.

"Let's head inside and see if things are back to normal."

As we approached the door, we could hear his telephone ringing. A wide grin hit Brettt's face and he yelled up into the sky.

"We hit the right note!"

About The Author

Mari Collier lives in the quirky town of Twentynine Palms. It's home to the largest Marine Training base in the nation and filled with art galleries and barber /beauty shops. She's a Director on the Board of the Twentynine Palms Historical Society, a member of the Desert Writers Guild, and Congregational Secretary for Good Shepherd Lutheran Church.

Her website is http://www.maricollier.com.

Lightning Source UK Ltd.
Milton Keynes UK
UKHW011823191120
373696UK00001B/161

9 781715 776442